FORBIDDEN VISION

Station Hill Contemporary Translations
edited by George Quasha

FORBIDDEN VISION

NINA BOURAOUI

TRANSLATED BY K. MELISSA MARCUS

STATION HILL

Published for Station Hill Literary Editions, a project of The Institute for Publishing Arts, Inc., a not-for-profit tax-exempt organization, by Station Hill Press, Inc., Barrytown, New York 12507.

Distributed by the Talman Company, 131 Spring Street, Suite 201E-N, New York, NY 10012.

Grateful acknowledgment is due to The National Endowment for the Arts, a Federal Agency in Washington, DC, and to the New York State Council on the Arts for partial financial support of this project. We also wish to thank the French Ministry of Culture and Communication for partial financial support assisting in the preparation of this translation.

Library of Congress Cataloging-in-Publication Data

Bouraoui, Nina
    [Voyeuse interdite. English]
    Forbidden Vision / by Nina Bouraoui.
      p.   cm.
    ISBN 088268177X
    I. Title.
    PQ2662.07755V6913   1995
    813' .914—dc20

                         95-16029
                            CIP

I

This morning the sun is higher. *Haughty* might be the word for it. Perched on an invisible throne, it pours its energy into my street that arrogantly shoots out from the rest of the city. It is here, at the epicenter of adventure, that everything happens for this woman, hidden behind her window, for that red-faced grocer sitting there on his footstool, for that man spying on a closed curtain, for those little boys and girls running around in a rectangle defined by dark and angular buildings.

People yell, they hang out, they stare, they cheat, they steal. And they rape. All the rest no longer has any existence; in the distance there is only a port without light animated by mournful sirens, a stopover between nothing and nothing, a gangplank thrown into the void whose end is known to none.

Without any effort I manage to extract something from the sidewalks, a gesture, a look, a situation that later gives me the lifeblood of the adventure. The imagination rides out on next to nothing, a window, a trolley, a little girl and her peculiar smile: then, spreading itself out right there in front of me, a new tapestry of stories woven out of words and wrongs which I invisibly mend with a coarse knot: lyricism. I'm no sucker for my vision of things. At my pleasure the stories travesty themselves, wrench themselves free from the banality of the really real, they reclaim themselves, change places with each other, and, once the mask goes on their strange unchanging faces, they give themselves up to the spectacle. The passerby crosses in front of wild jumping jacks of the imagination without so much as laying eyes on them. Coupling, things give birth to error, horror or beauty. It all depends. For the lunatic a sunny day can be icy and the rain burning!

Illusion works its infamous conjuring, passing from magic to the real with a hungry look and a sneering laugh worthy of Satan's mouth!

One day the lie rises up in rebellion inside your life. Hard to know. Indefatigable pendulum bumping between opposing spheres, it rebounds on the greater or the lesser truth, but it is always the window of the real that breaks first, and by our own game we get ourselves deported, on a voyage without a suitcase. My street is the underpinning of the adventure, the web, the grimy blackboard where the prose that gets inscribed remains indecipherable to the gawker. You have to take the time to observe, not just float along without seeing, not touch lightly without seizing, not gather without smelling, not cry without loving or hating. What matters is the story. To make a story for oneself before looking around at what's true. Real, unreal, what's the big deal! The tale surrounds the thing with a sudden glow, time deposits there one of its privileged attributes, memory, recall, or reminiscence, chance polishes the work and the thing takes form. And there at long last you have it, an adventure. What's there to tell if not a story?

I could never leave my street. I'm an integral part of it as I'm an integral part of these girls of the neighboring houses. Each night, taking turns, we faithful but nameless and faceless companions feed our souls with a new and strictly spiritual transport: the plaintive Moorish women send the murmur of their sameness back and forth between them, the hymn of common suffering. You have to be on your toes and wide awake to catch it in flight before it crashes below on the road that separates us.

A play of shadows, of lights and artful shades between clear and dark reveals the presence of young women hungering for events, framed by their windows, standing straight and serious behind the poplin cloth of closed curtains, they decorate the decayed buildings like statues erected to the glory of silence and private conversations; reduced to the state of inanimate stone, mute preachers, clandestine sentries, shrewd novices suspended by a divine thread above the roadway of fantasies, they defy men, desire and promiscuity. Temptresses, mockers, soul thieves, they are surrounded by interdictions and protected by a law which one cannot transgress, the anxious mother waits up, the dictatorial father commands: woe to he who will fix his eyes for too long on the feminine form silhouetted in the linings of the curtains! His eyes will transform into an old maid's genitals, unclean and forsaken, the blood will return to gush out of his sockets into the punctured white and, blinded by unreal forms, the man will die of his tainted tears. On his forehead, written in black, we will be able to read: *HARAM!*˙

Whom should we condemn? Whom should we pity the most? Men with roving and undiscriminating desire? City jackals, consciousness rapists, the acutely searching cyclopean eye, his tool a dart mounted on a radar space sweeper, feeling the blind angles by intuition, his arms dangling out of discouragement, his cumbersome and heavy genitals emptying onto him or his counterpart in front of a little girl both horrified and fascinated by the headless eyeless snail?

You slaves of sex, don't bother searching around, you'll never find that look of complicity — the veil you've thrown over things, thrown over your women can't just be ripped away!

And us young women? What are we doing all this time? This lost time! Phantoms of the street, cloistered animals, infantile women! Ungratified muses! Pardon me if I break down laughing! Protective of our senses and our beauty, we're bound to cultivate a false purity. Yes, I do say *false*. Come right along, men. Come have a little rest from your fruitless quest, repose a while on the hollows of our stomachs, come on over and admire the embryos of impurity germinating far from your caresses. Come smell the acrid perfume of vice and decadence scenting our soli-

---

*Haram: forbidden

tary and neglected gardens. Go to your windows and catch the dreams of Moorish women picturing a ballet of insatiable penises under their covers, as stinging as father's whip, as sharp as death's scythe.

Where's the indecency? In the street, behind our curtains or between the lines of the holy book? What's the origin of the big mistake? Does it come from nature who wanted to create nuance? Two ridiculously different sexes? And your hand reaching out for pussy, is it uglier than the wound that bleeds between our thighs? Who's the guilty one? A long deadened God, my mother under the body of my father, or You, peasants with your sewn-up vulvae? Whence the flaw in our civilization? From women jealous of their daughters, from men who haunt the capital square, or else from the verdict that comes in the end? Adolescents, you live in the shadow of a fatal declaration, your youth is a long trial that will finish in blood, a duel between tradition and your purity. Pure, too impure — frankly you don't measure up! Think of the heavy weight of time that tirelessly drags along in its hellish flood cycles of rules, customs, memories, reflexes and habits, torrents of mud in which your genitals are buried, already guilty at birth. Chasm of the innate and the *a priori!* Who has to pay? You, grandmothers who point the inquisitional finger, impurity-transgression detectives, you, "killjoys of pleasure," phony moralists, executioners obsessed with similarity, female thieves of ecstasy, obstructors of love? We, the exact duplicates of the first generation, passive and submissive sinners? You, sheet spotted with blood and honor? What takes shape in ruby ink mingled with your threads is the hope and the fear of mothers, fathers, men, the country and history itself.

Take a good look at our gangrenous souls. Try sounding out our spirits instead of burying your bitter and desiring selves in our hollow, this sucking and inspiring impasse! Yes, the body remains intact but good God, purity is not limited to a laughable little flow of blood! At night the curtain tears apart and I hear them, these starving hyenas, these so-called faces of virtue! The mucous covering rips from the movements of the spirit, and our groans flout the youth of the womanless street; poor males, poor old men, poor father, how I pity you!

A message? Sure. Come out of your lairs, stop wasting your time and ours, have the guts to turn tradition on its head, our morals and their values, rip off the curtains and the veils to bring our bodies together!

And a carnival of hands will break the windowpanes, will break the silence.

A bed with a single sunken spot, an earthenware pot without a flower, and a plain little clock with its large hand missing are my faithful companions in vigil. Persecuted by bloody nightmares, the darkness and the abnormal calm of the night, I doze in the artificial light poorly filtered by a yellowing lamp shade. The dusty cone of my nightlight lets only disobedient light rays escape, which waltz on the panes of my window before returning to smash themselves against the ceiling: the ultimate limit imposed on sleepwalking dancers. All day long I wander in solitude like a dog abandoned by his masters, his only enjoyment yanking on his chain so as to hurt even more! Hidden behind all manner of openings, I look, sound out, stare, in order to make the sublime ugly, the sun dark, the most complex situations ordinary, the richest ornaments poor. I count the trolley cars, the signs, the cars, the gawkers. I wait for the event, the blood, the death of a careless little girl or of a disoriented old man. I am the indiscreet eye hidden behind your enclosures, your doors, your keyholes, in order to unearth a fragment of Life which will never belong to me! I scrutinize my targets with a probe and a magnifying glass, I rip off clothes, make cuts in the skin, I dig right into the flesh, I dissect, take apart, separate, I bone the flesh and reglue the detached pieces, I carve into a point and resolder the whole thing when there is no more to discover, I make a "life-map" of internal organs wherein a biography worth perusing just might take shape; in short, I'm bored! My future is inscribed in the colorless eyes of my mother and in the monstrously formed bodies of my sisters: perfect incarnations of what will become of all cloistered women!

My dwelling has the calm of a seascape paneled in poisonous algae, the mutism of death; cast out from the surface, the murderous plants move about in silence, avoid touching each other, spit the fatal venom in the beautiful face of Life, then carry the mourning of their victim in disgrace. With this background grayer than my youth, I have become the shadow of a failed painting. Sadness is a living substance melded into the features of my face, an incredibly pointed chin plunges into a granular neck, my big indiscreet eyes fall on protruding bones, the skin of my cheeks is perfectly textured, though its color resembles a rotten pear. Bewilderment has contaminated the forms of my face, and I name my disgraces: evils of Beauty.

Invincible sadness! It makes time static like a block of lead that I collide with, rub up against, and wound myself with every day; coated with pitch, it oozes from the Almighty; malignant, it hardens on the floor of my room and on the walkways of the gangrenous city. Barring the way to little and big souls, changing the face of strength into a monkey grin named weakness, sadness renders me feeble, irritable, despairing, and deaf. It commands. I submit. Then everything falls down again. Light, desire and hope are dying in the bottom of a trash can under the unearthly garbage of the everyday. One must wait for all of this to be over, but the sadistic moments are not in a hurry; they get rid of each other in order to climb back up the course of time, going against the flow; tomorrow becomes yesterday, and today is but an intermediary between the same thing and the same thing.

Sadness gives me many words and many wrongs, I touch it with the ends of my fingers, and sometimes get a hold of it, I drink from its cup and it covers me with its unearthly wingspread, it breaks laws, scalps joy, it transforms the others into shadows, into imprints of shadows, into invisible filters, into

Blackness. The sterility of my existence germinated in the belly of my mother, and that of my little girls will germinate in mine. My poor daughters, how I pity you, I the faulted one who will give birth to you!

Women squeezed one against the other like fearful chickens cluck under the shelter of a bus-stop. A curious eye, twisted mouth, fidgety arm give life to packages of flesh bound by grayish veils; seen from my window, the one-eyed phantoms seem asexual, but if you observe them more carefully, you make out shapes, straining under the traditional dress, too fat to be masculine. They sneer, curse, insult under the little open window of the bus stop, they cover their faces in order to hide the childish joy at being there again, one more time, at the same hour, around this broken bench. Veils fall on light plastic sandals, wind themselves around the handle of an empty basket or twist between handbags with shiny buckles, the hardly lit up little torches turn around and around like fireflies awakened by the shadows of the women, farce of Life!

Connected to the sky by long metallic branches the trolley arrives bursting with people. Its antennae stretch out, fold up, then stabilize. The rubber springs connecting the two halves of the bus are stretched beyond endurance and when loosened resemble the old black skin of a horned animal. The doors open onto the street and mercilessly pour out a wave of passengers onto the asphalt. Pants, veils, red and black mops of hair try to untangle themselves in order to catch the step. But the women at the bus stop have already taken their place for another race. For a last time the driver roars the engine of the bus, while sponging the sweat off his uncovered head; the cruel doors close up again; children wedged between the two coaches and pressed together by a mobile arm laugh at the idea of falling.

sweat off his uncovered head; the cruel doors close up again; children wedged between the two coaches and pressed together by a mobile arm laugh at the idea of falling.

The trolley advances, blind and unsteady on its laid out path; the heads of the passengers glued to the windowpanes and iron casings resemble monsters, bottled for a long, a very long keeping, and the horrormobile penetrates deeper into the heart of the city where Life beats. The cheated passengers scatter out in my street; in front of the bus schedule the angry women loudly discuss the mistakes in the posted hours, readjust their veils and spit indignantly on the sidewalk which greeted them harshly only three minutes ago. Some women follow the blue monster with their eyes as it moves farther away from the stop; others, the corners of their lips set in rage, shake their fists in the air; the men run behind the indifferent machine, yelling, shouting incomprehensible sentences, mixing insults, prayers and slanders; children sneak away and cut through alleys running perpendicular to the normal path home in order to join up with it or get ahead, but the majority of them have already abandoned their smocks and book bags at the foot of a wall in order to participate in the games of the children of my neighborhood. With the help of "Gloria" milk cartons, the boys make their own soccer balls; plastic balls roll, dive, and burst in the gutter or under the foot of a clumsy person, setting off arguments which, though loud in word and gesture, nevertheless leave the men of my street indifferent.

I know them well, these male prisoners of the city; each has his reserved place, a laughable piece of false liberty! Clinging to the walls, hands spread out like fleshy fans encrusted in the stone, they observe three little girls piggyback on an orange plastic crate, playing with the feet of a table smashed to bits by time. Bathed in perspiration and unconsciously provocative, one of them capers around a ruptured pipemain; the diverted water whips her little child's legs; she lowers her head and intently observes the path of the water's jet which goes back up the curves of her thighs only to disappear under the folds of her flowered skirt.

The sun takes over the walls. The voyeurs put their heads together, make up their minds, then detach themselves with difficulty from the stone walls. They walk up and down looking for shade, showing their yellow teeth, grab their crotches in a show of power, and lean their backs up against the doorway of our house. I no longer distinguish anything but brown mops of hair; masculine armpits pour a sharp perfume into space, in a time all its own, intoxicating the children; the little girls continue to play around the pillars of vice; me, I stay crouched behind my window. There, a hidden spectator suspended above the city, I run no risks.

They are waiting for me. I've known it for a long time. From the tense hand of my mother, gripping mine when we went out, from her shoulders hunched over in order to hide the smallest feminine attributes, from her fleeing look in front of hordes of men congregated under the plane trees of the dirty city, I quickly understood that I must withdraw from this masculine country, this vast psychiatric asylum. We were among lunatics forever separated from women by the Moslem religion. They touched each other, squeezed each other, spit on the windshield of the cars or in their hands, lifted up old women's veils, urinated in the bus and caressed the children. They laughed out of boredom and despair.

In my turn, I lowered my eyes in front of the young boys who opened their flies when they saw us; my mother, mute, let five foreign fingers run over her body. We couldn't say anything, women who went out into the street were sluts!

The men lived in the year 1380 of the Hegira calendar; for us, it was the very beginning of the seventies. In the face of the growing anachronism of these men's lives, one had to come to a decision. Firm and definitive. Starting at puberty the females of the house had to live hidden behind the windows of a silent gynaeceum where time had lost its raison d'être. The hours flowed by slowly then ended up disappearing, destroyed by the unreality of our existence.

Our house is an inheritance from my grandfather, a well-known fresh fruit and vegetable merchant in the capital. Our neighborhood was once residential, but for a few years the slums have been coming our way and grafting themselves onto it; for lack of capital, the cisterns and sewage run-offs have never been maintained, which explains the horrible odor, like a corpse in an advanced state of decay, rising up from the sidewalks in the August heat. Lost amidst rubbish and the debris of buildings, set on top of this pile of garbage by I don't know what strange force, fitted with beautiful blue shutters attached to a flawless stone surface, my house on the outside contrasts with those next door.

The first floor is made up of a too-well-organized dining room, a colorless entryway and an only slightly disorganized little kitchen; the windows of the dining room are filled in by a wide single sheet, held in place by means of twelve tacks driven carefully into the wall paper. The first suras of the Koran are engraved on the doors of the Kabyle cabinets, on the copper tray cloths, and on the entire outline of the graphic design of a religious monument, occupying a place of honor above our heads in order to keep an eye on us. A woman's hand made of steel, warding off bad luck, is laid on a cloth sewn with an ornamental edge; the fringes of the main rug are carefully combed to the left; a stale kitchen odor has permeated walls, protective sheet, pouf pillows and cushions, and even the constant fresh air from the dining room can no longer get rid of it. Squatting, we eat around a low one-legged table; our crossed legs sometimes lightly touch each other, but no word, no look betrays the somewhat solemn silence forced upon us by the man of the house. A blue couch with imposingly large arms clashes with the multicolored wool of the carpets and rugs covering the tilework. The style of our Southern wools is characterized by multiple colors: ochre, yellows, reds, orange, reddish browns similar to kaleidoscopic images slightly dulled by the lack of natural light.

Our rooms, all precisely square and without the least trace of color, resemble each other; a chestnut-colored blanket serves as a bedspread, a sheepskin as a bedside rug, a curtain with no longer very fresh looking flowers hides the little bathroom, the windows are narrow but adequate. In spite of the austerity, some signs however give a personal touch to each of our cells: Zohr always keeps her holy book on the night stand, along with a bottle of ninety percent strength alcohol, a roll of gauze-tape, and a jar of henna; Leyla, she has buried all of her belongings in a small plaid suitcase: old bills, pebbles, cloth scraps, and dust fill her little suitcase that no one dares open, so dirty and secret it seems. My parents' room has an extra cupboard, and a commode scratched on the top, and the bed is wider and more sunken in than ours.

Above my writing table, a female swimmer in a period piece bathing suit is stuck on the wall. A wooden frame surrounds the flesh sculpture, frosted petals gilding its edges, but if one looks more closely it is in fact the water from a previous dive, running over her skin.

There's a winter garden near my room. Paradoxical, you will think, in this country where heat is never lacking! Originally, the winter garden was a beautiful sunny terrace; one fine morning, my father decided on his own to condemn it. His motive? Men in the street could catch a glimpse of us! With their dry stalks, pretending to be brave guardians, the plants of the dusty greenhouse are like miniature monsters who persist in living on a measly half-glass of water a day. Weeds and dead leaves wrap themselves around withered roots waiting in vain for the life-giving sun to appear. No hope, poor plants! My mother doesn't even bother sneaking around anymore to pull out the few flowers that might make it to the end! Frightened by what one commonly calls the things of nature, daily and remorselessly she goes after the miserable buds of color. Note well! The floral fornication could give me ideas! In spite of her thirteen births out of which ten human things not of this world disappeared in the dark galleries of the plumbing, sex is a cursed flower planted between Satan's two horns! And the height of irony is she'll be right beside me on my bloody wedding night. Perpetrator of a terrible plot, she will wait, anxious, behind the door of the bridal chamber, for the honorific tearing, to flatter nothing but her pride as a mother. She will listen for my smallest sighs, my smallest tremblings, and then will drum on the door, too impatient to show off the stained sheet, infallible sign of my perfect upbringing. And the family ululations will mix with the cries of joy of a mother entrusting her offspring to a stranger. Murderous Mamma!

In the dining room, the windows closed as usual, my family prepares to have lunch. I recognize myself in these faces, their hardness accentuated by wan complexions and overly black hair, these milky bodies dressed in white and maroon moving about silently in the semi-darkness of a hellish scene behind closed doors. Languid movements conspire to retain a semblance of utility; they keep busy, bustle wordlessly around the table or in front of the silent TV; I hear the noises of plates, silverware, the kitchen faucet strangled by its gaskets, a chair pulled out, but not a word. The women of the house have renounced frivolity and seduction; barefooted or in thongs, they are unimportant piles of fat floating about in scarcely becoming dresses, or bodies with missing forms, always close to vanishing; irrevocable errors that nature should have had mercy on; cancerous conscripts, they are the ghosts of my sleepless nights!

Squatting behind a low table, my older sister Zohr waits for the mint tea to steep. The twisted spout of the tea pot sends a stream of vapor bouncing off the table before it comes and dies on her face; the column of transparent water doesn't even make her eyes wink, they are so deeply set, sunken in the black and deep hollows of the empty looking sockets. The "buttonholes" hide two nervous, almost-white pupils, which seem to stare momentarily at the little game of the pouring spout.

Always pulled back in a crooked and washed-out colored braid, weakened by ribbons tied too tight, today Zohr's hair falls in unequal strands onto her conspicuously veined body. Made of a single block out of which one hardly distinguishes the profile of her face, Zohr's miserable body has been amputated from the two majestic sculptures innocently put into our care by God.

Every evening she tightens a carefully made corset of bandages in order to mask two breasts whose unsupported nipples suffocate behind the band of cloth closed by a diaper pin, itself lodged in the ridiculous groove separating the two buds that will never reach full growth. She only undoes her corset so she can rub her back-like torso whose shoulder blades are probably marked by two brown stains, sticking out in a puzzling way. Reddened by the gauze knotted flush with the skin, this trunk remains straight, however, without ever betraying the perfectly horizontal line of the legs joined to a hipless pelvis. Sitting like this, thoughtful and patient, her bosom, fighting against a backbone that would like to adapt itself to this uncomfortable posture, doesn't bend. Zohr is engaged in a battle against her nature, her feminine nature, a rotting thing for our father, shame for our offending mother; it is she, the traitor, who pushes Zohr further in her sacrifices, her artifices and her grotesque cover-ups. And in our presence, the fake never forgets to pinch her slightly fleshy mouth, once it has relaxed, to hide it, to bite it until it bleeds, to finally destroy this piece of red scratched flesh, sign of life and fecundity!

I remember neither our childhood games, nor the complicity of our laughter nor the youthful pranks; no, I remember only the fusion of our respective sadness. With a strange agility, her large hands, stretched to death by indefinitely long fingers, ran over my face, puffed up by sobs and despair. She squeezed me against her with a man's roughness in order to pull out, taste, and absorb my distress, as if hers had not yet reached its paroxysm, the limit of the unavoidable and of no return!

She detected my slightest signs of weakening: a frozen smile, a tight jaw, slightly quivering lips, a distant look, for she knew better than anyone the suffering of being born a woman in this house: a stain who would later become a slut. In admiration before my tears she pressed her cheeks to mine, drooping and irritated by the flow, then withdrew with a brief smile of satisfaction, the skin of her face streaked with small grooves of salt. Then I had the feeling of thievery, of illicit misuse beyond the constraints of reason; I felt robbed, worse yet: ridiculed. In "appropriating" my tears and newly manifested sufferings, Zohr, in my eyes, incarnated all of the misery of human nature; I saw in her my gloomy destiny, and my tears multiplied; coming up from the bottom of my throat, they crossed the interior of my face and arriving at the orbital opening spread uncontrollably over the covering of their source. When Zohr huddled in front of me, I always feared that the two ends of her silhouette would come apart. My imagination allowed me to hear the noise of her ribs crumbling at each unusual movement, her tissues compressing, her entrails punctured by knee bones, making a grinding sound; her head in the void, she took hold of one of her lanky arms and heaved it behind her shoulder. There, a little pile of formless flesh, she let out the last cry of an animal awaiting its death in solitude; but Zohr was unaware that Death was already in her. There was no point in calling her, Death spoke in her place and fed on her little remaining flesh. Death had chosen its mask, and unknowingly Zohr transported it throughout the house and slept in its arms. She looked Death up and down in her mirror, and her inexplicable tremblings were in fact the hidden derisive laughter of the grinning skull.

Death slowly poured its poisoned lymph into the body of my sister so that she could appreciate it each day of her youth; Death had frozen her blood, hardened her veins and drawn cracks at the corner of her mouth in indelible ink; four sparkle-shaped wrinkles stretched her eyes, and under her neck hung a ruddy new skin, cut in the middle by two ropes of white mucous membrane.

Our father is sitting on a prayer rug whose colors are too vivid for a holy carpet. The word "God" written in large wool letters vomits its sinuous calligraphy unto the impious. Imprisoned in a starch-stiffened robe, the somber-eyed male who sired me waits for his meal. Two red initials indiscreetly stain his hard collar. His head held high, he is careful not to let himself develop slovenly habits. No suspicious form soils the whiteness of his indoor apparel. He constantly pulls up his socks in order to hide milky, almost transparent, hairless calves. When he manages to trap the elastic above his knees, he sighs briefly, relieved, then thrusts his well-manicured hands into a small bowl of fruit. Dotted with little dilated pores, his fingers feel out a bunch of muscat grapes. The sugar-swelled grapes roll, slip, then squish under the pressure of the thumb and forefinger, filed down to the bloody quick and whose well-pushed-back skin highlights the roseate half-moons that entirely invade the rounded tips. Black curls, cut very short, undulate on his temples, then reappear in a fine mustache laid in place with the help of a few drops of vetiver; the forehead shoots down into a horizontal crease lodging two dark brown chestnut eyes, encircled by whites as shiny as a new piece of pottery; they stare at one of the disemboweled grapes which spits out its juice and its seeds onto the edge of the low table. With its transparent and delicate skin, the hollowed out fruit resembles my adolescent genitals; attached to the main branch by two smaller branches which could be my legs, it empties its flesh in front of my father. Two years. It's already been two years that he no longer speaks to me. Two long years during which my body has not stopped oozing out impurity. And it continues! My deformed breasts hurt me, two hollows have modified the shape of the small of my back, under my arms a fragrant shadow becomes blacker and blacker; in vain I wash myself, dress my cyclical "wounds" and shave the hair of my most intimate being, I remain dirty and unworthy of his word; I am an articulated scarecrow, a female with rotted sexual organs that must absolutely be ignored so as to escape divine condemnation!

That night he wasn't sleeping either, I heard him walking behind the door of my room. An almost palpable event had, by its very presence, inundated the air, the walls, the ground of our dwelling. I felt the fever progressively invading me, a bellows irritated my ears, convulsions mixed with inexplicable heat overwhelmed my body: the metamorphosis was soon to make its appearance on the flesh stage. Zohr screamed under her covers; outside, the cars had stopped moving; unwarranted car honking covered the cries of a cruel mother leaning out her window. The walls of my room smelled like a corpse. The men conversed very loudly. They brutally opened and closed the doorway of our house; one of them had slipped into the small garden, and, waiting, made himself the secret accomplice of my father. A lost little girl, crying over her misery, I had neither the strength nor the courage to reach my window. I wrapped my thighs with my sheet, very quickly blistered with red. My entire body was drooling. A stranger was slashing my genitalia from the inside, I was transforming into a monstrous insult, and I prayed to God with all of my powers so that he would stop this disgraceful and shameful flow!

I led myself toward my bathroom to try to erase the first marks of the dreaded impurity, but it was too late. My father appeared suddenly in my room. In fury, he clutched his head between his hands. Naked, my legs hindered by the sheet of crime, I fell to his feet and pleaded that I was not responsible; by opening my veins nature had risen up against me; henceforth my heart beat in my lower abdomen, its arteries like gargoyles on a rainy day went beyond my suppurating flower and poured out onto my thighs all of their hate and violence.

He beat the daylights out of me and said: "Female, fuck, femininity, fornication, feebleness, flaws, start with the same letter." These were his last words.

The kitchen door is open, and an odor of stuffed peppers seizes my throat. A tray placed on the floor waits for condiments; my mother clangs the pans to assure me of her presence. I look at her from behind. She swings her flesh package in all directions, right, left, high, low, her posterior seems to be animated by an inner force. Her stomach remains immobile and rests from its innumerable births on the kitchen sink crowded with dishes, plates, and knives. A piece of Life stuck in the pouch of the female who bore me seems to hurt! A pipe leaks, a sponge spits its foam onto the baked clay wall, it is hot and humid in the blinding darkness of the little kitchen.

Dear Mamma, why must we always look at you from behind? Is it your usual posture or rather the cowardice of not facing up to us? Yet, it is very much from the front that you conceived me! Ah! how unruly like a bad girl memory is! I would so much like to remember your kisses, your caresses, an embrace, the warmth of your big mistreated breast, my throat sucked you in, and you must have screamed; I would like to remember, too, your face when you saw me for the first time. My eyes are not what you looked at, no, you quickly spread apart my legs to see whether a piece of skin pointed out of my scarcely formed body! Happiness doesn't depend on much! Three seconds to see and to know, a glance between my thighs, a feeling finger, and you decided, by your tears or your cries of joy, my life, my destiny, and my death!

The disappointment was great! Pardon me Mamma, how I understand today your distress in the face of my chest which would have to enlarge. You did well not to wipe my tears, I was a false promise who nourished itself on you even before I knew you! Keep your back to me, above all! I am not a beautiful sight: my hair is long, my limbs are delicate, and nothing moves under my tunic!

You? I guess that in your middle is a gaping hole, a big open eye whose bruised edges no longer exist, a dried up crater which does, however, remember its fires and its earliest, rarely fruitful flows. Mine resembles the stretched out mouth of a drowsy young dog, still clenched tight, pink on the outside like the body of a newborn, sticky inside like the cord that used to connect us.

Where is our natural attachment dying now? In the bottom of a trash can, in the open lot of an amnesiac memory or under the hollow of your guilty belly?

Nothing remains of it for me but a button of chubby skin, endlessly reminding me of our first meeting. Our first separation.

I have seen my father go after these two big breasts full of veins and regrets which hung down; in spite of savage quarrels, his mouth, wide open, tried to swallow up one of the nervous sacks of the female who bore me, but he immediately spat it out, his two jaws unable to hold the totality of the piece of skin marked on the surface by a brown halo. A nap had left me thirsty, so I went to the kitchen to fetch a glass of water when I surprised them, there, sprawled on the tile flooring. The two silhouettes merged on the floor seemed anonymous to me at first, they were no longer in their usual place. Forming a single block, animated on the sides by four very agitated limbs, one would think that it was a fat and puffing seasquirt thrashing on the bank; panting, gasping, it recovered itself, drooled on what suddenly became unfamiliar ground to me! My father had tucked up his robe, his little calves bound by black socks miserably tapped out the rhythm; cornered between the heavy and not very agile thighs of my mother, he gripped this rowboat as well as he could, bellowing like a trapped animal. Very small, very delicate, very black, he resembled a worm digging his hole in an arid and bushy earth; under him, the bushy ground shook and dug its venomous thorns into the bit of exposed flesh.

He rolled, rebounded, banged against these forms, which he had himself rendered inhuman; his head buried under an armpit where reddish brown lace hung, invented for itself a more desirable and less fatiguing body. Full of unsatisfied desires, he took vengeance on my mother's stomach by administering to her regular and violent hits with a hidden weapon which he alone held. The statues had quit the frigidity of their building material; underneath the stone, two organs filled up with blood. Blood similar to that which sometimes reddened my inexperienced sex.

The victim folded back up her monstrous thighs. Her hair spread out on the tiling like a wolf's head disheveled by the dust took the form of an open sea urchin, her legs were tossed about in all directions and had hardly the force to set themselves upright in order to shine under the electric bulb of the ceiling fixture. After a last jolt which shook the entire house, my father pulled himself out of the viscous trap, then scoured his hands with a household sponge. The female who bore me was nothing more than a vulgar untied package, the surprise that it held was a bad joke! Nothing lived under the cloths and the silkpaper, there was just a bottomless pit with rough and uncomfortable walls. My father wiped off his hands as he strolled about the kitchen. His ruffled mustache poked up above his shining mouth. I had just enough time to hide behind the couch. There, I was not at risk. I saw without being seen my poor mother stretched out on the tiling, her stripped parts slowly became covered with bruises. My father was talking loudly. Oh yes! He held a grudge against these deformed genitals that never really satisfied him. To finish off his hardly complimentary speech, he waved his kitchen towel and violently whipped her. It always happened like that when

25

my mother gave birth. She had hardly the time to recover from a terrible disappointment when my father inflicted on her all of his lack of understanding and roughness. What then? Not a child but an aftertaste of powerlessness blocked the throat of the male who sired me; for more than an hour he had tried to spit his desire into this unfathomable body, but finally, fatigue and disgust got the better of him. My mother said nothing, too weary, also too used to it to defend herself; the "inter-course" wide open, her thighs lifted up, she seemed to wait for the first convulsions of the birth! Very often, she begot nothing but death. A shriveled up skin hung at the end of the umbilical cord like the hardly appetizing bait of an old fish hook! The child she carried aged in her stomach and only came out for the funeral.

The funeral was brief. My mother wrapped the offspring with newspaper and shut the garbage can lid on the little gaping head with its half-closed eyes; when the child was but an egg cracked by an impatient little finger, she was satisfied to submerge it in the toilet bowl. Around the little beast the water formed swirls then carried it away toward a countryside of big black pipes from which it alone knew the exit.

Only three girls survived, three little very slippery sprouts who cried out, their feet still cornered between the caved-in and blood-dripping bricks of the deadly well. To remedy the weighty absence of male children, my mother called upon an old woman who had the gift, so it was said, of healing this dangerous anomaly.

Wrenched from her faraway mountains, the healer lived under our roof for several days. Her awakening marked the end of my fits of insomnia. I turned off my little bedside lamp and spied: the slow steps of a Kabyle sorceress with arms that sing under the tingling of jewelry, the rustling of fabric impeding the solitary walk of the mystic in movement, surprised looks in front of the faucets and their multiple functions, odor of goat and dampened herbs. A rarely combed mop stuck out like bad tempered snakes from the ineffective swirls of a royal blue turban, her face half-covered by a cotton mask was marked from the forehead to the chin by irregular green lines, pointed on the bridge of the nose, drawn out around the edge of the mouth, non-existent in the shadow lodged between the face and the throat, and I found them larger, more vulgar, on all the phalanxes of her fingers and in the lattice designs of her open palms.

On each step of the staircase her body poured bitter perfumes, acidic or peppered; without seeing her, I guessed her morning route step by step, the filth wove a rug of heavy and persistent odors on the ground; like a thread stretched between her bedroom and her hair, the perfume of her body led me to her; on the second floor her veil spread an odor of rotting meat, five sweaty fingers had gripped the landing, I found a black fingernail there; further on, her armpit had emptied itself against a wall; once arrived downstairs, my face become powdered with henna and I discovered the breath of her sigh; I ended up closing my eyes and no longer thought but with my nose, it led me well, I walked with my head slightly bent so as to lose nothing, and the most intimate scents marking my nostrils persisted until bedtime.

Prognathic, she could never entirely close her mouth, beneath our eyes, a jagged cave containing more than a treasure shamelessly displayed its hiding places, its nooks and crannies plugged up by yellowish residues. The old sorceress sharpened her thirty-two little pieces of ivory with a brown stick waved about during her hollow incantations; intrigued by the inopportune presence of a fragment of nature in the sterilized house, one day I sniffed the dry stake in the hope of finally knowing the sweet scent of a piece of wood born under the sun, when, floored by the foul emanations of a deceitful piece of wood, I perceived my naiveté. Innocently I was deeply breathing in the gray gums, the greenish teeth, the lose tooth stumps, the swollen palate and the suppurating tonsils of the sorceress! Then I threw up my morning milk.

The healer ground herbs in an earthenware cup filled with semolina, she moistened the grain with so-called sacred water and with lukewarm urine, added two thick drops of milk and then boiled the contents. My mother, her legs spread, perched above the vitreous mix, with the grimace of effort on her face. Comic scene ... such a little pot for an overweight body, dark smoke to stir up the faith, and a chant from the mountain to cure the sick goat! The ameliorating vapors penetrated the inner thighs of the female, reappeared as transparent pearls on her forehead, then undulated on the exposed folds of fat. The old Kabyle begged her God to give to this poor creature, my mother, the power to finally create a penis and then undertook a wild dance: the first sign of the trance. Her turban flew about to the other side of the room, thus freeing the mop which took the opportunity to breathe; she showed her jutting gums suddenly covered with white foam, her two arms lifted toward the sky banged one against the other, and the music of the coral bracelets became even more forceful. The veil caressed my anxious mother, dipped into the magic mixture and ended up falling at the feet of the healer, then other less ample veils, more gay, wrapped around the waist and imposing torso of our guest; they could not fall; held by a belt of small silver bells, they were content to follow the abrupt movements ordered by God.

Thanks to a very clever way of leaning her weight on her hip, no smoke curl escaped from my mother's chasm; she applied herself, closed her eyes, stretched out her hands toward the healer and sometimes even grabbed her crotch with a faith which I didn't know she possessed; I understood at this precise moment the very real frustration of this woman. Yes, she wanted a boy, but she wanted even more than that. Weighted down by her breasts, her thighs, her pelvis, her abdomen, my mother desired a penis all for herself, a penis that she would keep all her life, and with that, finally, she would be respected. If it had been able to burst forth from her lower abdomen at the time of the incantations, she would have been a fulfilled woman, and who knows, maybe even worshipped!

We girls were her pain, our faces, our bodies reminded her of her weakness, our sex recalled her own amputated sex, and if she always had this sad air it was because she knew of the absurdity of our existence apart, which distanced us from men and our counterparts a little more each day. Seized by a sudden humility, I got down on my knees on the tilestone of regret, and, for the first time, I began to pray with her.

The woman from the Atlas mountains left us, forgetting her promises, her trances and her dry stick. We all waited; then, one morning, hope vanished; we stopped waiting and life began its normal course again, cut off from patience and illusions. The dry stick sleeps under my pillow. When the desire for evil attacks me, I sniff with delight the old odors of a dirty mouth, brush my teeth with the stake which likes to entrench itself in the hollow of my cheeks; it rips the carmine colored and aphthous mouth, penetrates into the darkest crevices, plants its shards in my gums, and then a burning pain bursts forth accompanied by fresh blood, intoxicating because of its salt, exciting because of its unusual course. I let it run as it wants to on my lips, my throat, my neckline, and it dries like a piece of liquefied laundry on the hard and pointed rock of my jagged nipples. Drunken with evil, I then wash my mouth with a throatful of musk perfume and the alcohol digs more deeply into my still open wounds.

Silence, solitude, the final abandonment of real Life submerge me with an inhuman fear; the others are quiet, the walls close in, my body is at the point of rotting. I feel the hardening of my organs, and all by itself my heart decides a new tempo: the faint music of death. Pushed by the instinct for survival I chase away decadence with decadence; evil and illness complete unto themselves abruptly turn toward the good; and with the pain of the forbidden I awaken my body, at point of death save it from the fall, cover it with murderous thoughts and give birth to myself!

II

Always down on four paws, nosing in the garbage cans like a little animal searching for bones and food scraps, black hair with ash curls, brown pimples and greedy mouth, her arms held out toward someone known only to herself, immersed in stories of little girls whose idols we will never be, inveterate complainer, bulimic dressed in dirty sweaters and shod in noisy old worn out shoes, wild child often hidden under the stairs, behind the kitchen door or in her bed, Leyla is my second sister. Horrified by the arrival of another girl, my mother wanted to throw her from the window without even looking at the two big intelligent eyes which, in an instant, grasped the undesirable presence of their owner. Finally, human reason had the day, making of Leyla a person miraculously saved from the sidewalk. We let her battle with life, alone, spread out on the couch, hoping that she wouldn't make it. A formal interdiction against touching her. A glass of milk spilled on her gluttonous mouth, bouillon dirtied her underwear . . . . Very quickly, animated by an inexplicable need to mother, the guilty female took her under her arm again, swinging her to and fro between the kitchen and the dining room, the laundry room and the upstairs rooms; the soapy housecleaning water moistened the skull of the little fallen angel and ended up drowning her mind; she grabbed onto the stools in order to walk; but her two bowed out legs were unable to hold her up, and she fell again, shamefaced, forever nailed to the ground.

She has never spoken. Only a kind of grunting. Sometimes she lifts her eyes toward us, her tender look moistened by tears heavy with meaning, but finding no one to see it shine, it reaches the bleached ground: her lifelong companion.

She eats with her fingers, keeps count of the kicks received, registers only rarely a helping hand, hardly ever a laugh, a few distancing dreams inside a warm abdomen rocked by blood and lymph, bathing in the curious seascape of the placenta. Little thing so far from us, little indifferent animal, little miserable thing! Where do you come from with your forever-flowing saliva and these odd hands with more fingerprints than mine? A bump at the end of her nose, two ears round as the handle on a mug and curved eyes give her a look all her own: the slight madness of betrayed innocence.

I never play with my little sister, sometimes we caress each other, she nuzzles up against me and pretends to be asleep again, our hearts answer each other with irregular beats, and I let the dialogue of our flesh do its work. What could I say to her? What more could she know? Yes, we're killing time. We await further boredom in another house with yet other windows for looking out at the trees, the street, the men, the world. Separately. I am but bare skin with carnassial teeth, gnawing the silence, in silence; I hide my wounds, smother my cries, I am cowardly and passive, no taste for rebellion, pity or compassion. I am waiting. That's all. A growth, one more of my little sister's enemies. The ghost of a shadow!

I like to thrust my fingers into the grease waterfall that forms waves of milk on her stomach. When my index finger runs down the length of her little spinal column, indented like that of the sea horse, her eyes color to yellow, her throat transforms into the humming of a busy anthill, and I feel her blood roar under her skin like the pulp of the blood orange; once satisfied, the little slut leaves my arms for Zohr, but our older sister's door is always locked. Like a sacred tomb, her room is forbidden to us, we only have the right to a few whiffs of alcohol escaping from between the tight floorboards. That's all. And Leyla screams louder, but no one hears her. Only Ourdhia was capable of calming our little monster. Ourdhia, a native of the red earth of the desert, good at everything, at cleaning everything, filling the emptiness in everything. A mystical aura encircled this woman's being. Like an opaque veil surrounding her forms, fragile, delicate, perfumed by rock and alpha waves, her aura, so present, pierced me and I sunk into a guelta* where time had interrupted its inevitable march forward, its desire to touch the end of its unfathomable function. She was always there to offer some small amounts of tenderness, and I sucked on her empty breast during the storm, buried my head in her hollow stomach; through her I escaped the cursed night, I captured the strange warmth of a long body whose skin, cracked in the most tender places, wet my face with the mists of a far-away region; with two little arms I squeezed all of the grandeur of a country whose inhabitants have not destroyed the soul of natural edifices; rocked by hands and voice softer than those of my mother, I fell asleep far from my room and my boredom. Yes, Mother, I admit that I preferred her to you. I remember her arrival well, she wore a dress draped around her waist, pulled up under her armpits, undone in the back. The blazing color of its cubic patterns, the perfect form of the shoulders and hips made one forget the poor quality of the worn-out crumpled cloth. Traveler without a suitcase, Ourdhia's only baggage was her revealing smile of sadness and her new pride at being a city dweller.

She had rung at our door by chance, explaining that she was hungry, thirsty, needed shelter for a conscientious and undemanding mind. My mother, who had just borne her young, accepted. Ourdhia carried out her household tasks with a seriousness approaching mania, slowing down on the floorboards, the bottoms and tops of things, the nooks, the crannies, the inside of the cupboards, of the chests, and to round off her work she emptied our souls of their dust and their boredom. She cleansed my heart of its anxieties, wrapped up our childhood illnesses, swept away

---

*guelta: waterhole

doubt, nightmares, erased the black shadows from our faces, cleared away sadness and scoured morose thoughts. Since speaking was forbidden in our house, Ourdhia for her part seemed deaf and dumb, but I quickly perceived that her muteness had nothing to do with ours: discretion was her only wealth. She kissed dry bread before throwing it away, thanked water for flowing in waves and lowered her eyes when we stared at her too insistently. I liked to watch her work. She seemed to be armed with a superhuman force, things had a new shine, food another taste and even her prayers carried the seal of purity. Thanks to her I would enter an unreal but benevolent world: the world of the Imaginary. As a child nightfall was my worst enemy; the natural light would disappear with the sun, then out of the rectangular glass windows of the neighboring houses loomed a sickly light filtered by the curtains or squarely cut into horizontal lines by the wood of the grooved shutters. What I'd do was hit the light switch, then my room always seemed more suffocating as the objects drew nearer to each other, united by a single beam of light, dulled by the opaque bulb whose two metallic filaments vibrated at the least movement. Assaulted by the seeds of perversion which I avoided concentrating on, and especially kept from understanding, my mind froze in fear, my face smothered beneath the pillow; when the multicolored forms began to waltz under my eyelids I called Ourdhia, always ready to calm childhood anguish. She would sit on the edge of my bed, one hand placed on my forehead, the other on my heart, and recount to me the strange tale of the desert. She spoke calmly; under her hand my heart threw out hardly noticeable little regular beats as a sign of my appreciation. Thump, thump, a drop of blood tickled her brown palm, our skin alone separated us. Ochre light flooded my room, I forgot the light switch, the yellowish string attached to its lampshade, the exhausted bulb no longer existed. Two boulders had burst through at the foot of my bed, a soft breeze raised my curtains; behind the window a salt pond blistered with lunaria flowers was forming; under the door three roses were beginning to grow; fossilized in the grains of sand, as fragile as glass, they slid their sand petals in between the floorboards and perfumed my room with a new fragrance. The desert was really there. My dressing room was smothering beneath a generous block of sand: the dune. Its crest caved in beneath the footsteps of a man in black who disappeared behind my little mirror, continuing his walk alone with the aid of a staff. The entire countryside passed through me, a round flat cake was cooking at my feet, my fingers picked through a sand rosary, and I felt a thousand little mirages shimmering on my body. It was fresh and dry. The desert was really there. In the distance, the dancing Turaeg could be seen through the flames of an encampment, two eyes underlined with kohl surveyed the night while camel's milk flowed from a slit goatskin bottle. The palm grove opened up to me, the crickets, earth's crayfish, gripped the bucket chain and one by one dived into the only well to rinse their throat with an exhausting song.

My nomad, you see I say my nomad, belonged to a big Turaeg tribe dispersed throughout a country with no apparent borders where beauty was the worst of dangers. It intoxicated men, women, forcing them to go always further, always higher, to the extreme side of the sun. Yes, desert drunkenness exists. Ourdhia has encountered it. Hunger was often the cause of meeting someone again, the Turaeg stayed in the oasis for a few days, then fatigued by the "greenness," the almost drinkable water and the incessant song of the cicadas ensconced at the foot of the date trees, they began once again to wander; sometimes crossing the path of an animal carcass, escaping insect stings and fear, indulged at night by the cries of a desperate hyena, they crossed the hostile earth perhaps with the aim of taming it. But beauty does not allow itself to be softened easily; insolent, it burns by day, disappears at night, and in the early morning hours emerges haughty and distant, virgin and inviolable. Accomplice of a murderous sun that has engraved the initials of effort and solitude on the faces of the Turaeg, beauty is found in the most barren of regions, empty of shadows and footsteps, there where it alone reigns.

Ourdhia had refused escort in her walk through nature. The desert listens to itself alone; with luck, between two silences, you can catch a noisy moment: the sun diving into moving sand.

Guided by the stars, she had reached the most naked region, beauty without show, the essence of the sublime: the Tenere. Emptiness of emptiness, absolute of absolute, center of the earth, epicenter of nothingness, this place finally crowned the disciplined walk of the nomad, there she communed with the truth. The Tenere, vast empire of sand, is represented on my map by a wide yellow stain. But I knew nothing. Ourdhia taught me. The Tenere possessed a single tree, an intruder. Sole point of reference for men and animals, enigmatic presence in the inhumanity of the desert decor. A tree whose bare branches emitted no sound, an imposing trunk disheveled on top by slender rough branches; in spite of the drought, the temperature extremes, the dryness of the climate and the devastating sand, the tree lived on. For centuries. Alone. In silence. One night, men from the city in an elevated truck crashed into this insolent presence. It never grew again. In that brief moment the Tenere lost the unique manifestation of its soul. In its place a chestnut shadow has dug into the sand. The sun remembers. Out of respect it dare not light up the bare tomb. Neither flower nor prayer, just a dark imprint that can't be found on my map.

Ourdhia took care of the errands. Because she was a foreigner, my mother didn't think of her as a woman, more than anything else she was the maid; so much for the noble carriage of her head, her delicate joints and her princess face; henceforth her bleach-soaked fingers closed the trash cans and scrubbed the toilets. Optimistic, the nomad carried a basket and a net bag for her things. I envied her, desert walker now citydweller, she alone had the right to leave the prison. Observation became a true art. Nothing escaped me. I minutely scrutinized the course that the nomad would take, each person whose path she would cross, and I guessed all of her gestures, even the most unexpected.

The signal? The noise of the front door, and, suddenly, uncertainty in full daylight. At the beginning, everything went fine, her teeth held the traditional veil in place, Ourdhia never covered her head, only her shoulders: first signs of a perfect body able to stir up the desires of these men who were always in heat. Her bearing was proud, her basket stayed wedged in her slightly bent wrist. When she passed under my bedroom she paused just slightly. She alone knew. Then the men of my street started to gather, and the illusion of liberty was soon to disappear. The city seemed to be a bell jar closing little by little onto her shoulders; I saw a dark wall being erected at the end of the alley; men, mangy dogs, wandering children waited for her at the corner, as if nothing were happening she continued her walk, proud and light. Even the sun hid its face so as not to take part in the preparations for the sad show, he, witness of her first steps and of true beauty, how could he have continued to light up a sordid street even more dangerous than poisonous insects? He shrugged his shoulders, and with the help of some clouds, turned toward the Atlas peaks. The children had stopped playing, the little girls knew, and like me they didn't warn her of the danger. She walked faster, the basket swung to and fro between the empty space and her thigh, the veil shrank, so did the sidewalk with it. On the way a ruptured drainage pipe sprayed her, sad city. Suddenly, she stopped dead. A snotty-nosed kid threw a rock at her, another, more courageous, spit right in her face, two young men let their disgusting hands run over her beautiful body. I was screaming. She alone knew. The growing din of the city covered her cries, yes, Ourdhia was defending herself, she wasn't afraid, but what can be done in the face of these unleashed hordes? Ourdhia was a woman, and even more, oh! desolation, she was black!

"Kahloucha! Kahloucha! Kahloucha! Kahloucha! Kahloucha! Kahloucha! Kahloucha!*" The deadly word rang out all over the city, the syllables detached from each other, stronger each time, they banged against her temples, low pitched, high, shrill, muffled, piercing, they unceasingly found a different echo: the windows, the cafes, the bus stops, the plane trees reverberated the insult, the car metal added rhythm to the plot, and under the earth resonated a genuine groaning — mine.

---

*Kahloucha: Negress

She left us with no explanation. One morning, her mattress was folded in two, her veil, usually hung behind the door of the laundry room, had disappeared, and the dust cloth was carefully put on the kitchen table, with a sad air it waited for her replacement. The last images from a dream were still attached to the curtains, the room smelled like the bed, the sheets, the hasty and rash departure, the sink had kept one of her hairs as a souvenir: as a question mark fissuring the white ceramic, on the tiling, the imprint of her steps, on her night table, an envelope folded in four was addressed to me. It contained a metallic object. I knew. Ourdhia had left me her Southern Cross, four pink stones gleamed at the end of each branch. I was crying. Her smell disappeared as the days went by, I could not keep hold of it. But now I remember a mixture of amber, musk and licorice.

Poisonous plants, bedridden child, malignant outgrowths, warts gifted with reason, pathetic people contaminated by boredom and sadness, this is my family. In this distressing painting, in which the painter has emphasized the colors of despair, I have my place between two walls, under a window, my back to a rickety chair. Oh! I'm hardly any better than the other characters! Grainy from head to foot, the bones of my wrists jutting out too much, my neck encircled by three rings of useless skin, I don't feel very pretty. Old adolescent, worn out before my time, my silhouette and my face didn't stay faithful to my childhood photos, only the eyes are intact with an additional shadow pleasantly recalling their ink black. Nanny goat with overgrown hair who plays with her hoof while waiting to be torn from the herd for the slaughterhouse, I live my youth on the razor's edge, one false step, a single sign and I'm ready for the event. Following the family mania, I'm starting to hide my breasts by holding myself in a slightly bent position, my ribs pulled in and my arms shielding me. The body is the worst of traitors, without asking the opinion of the interested party, it stupidly delivers undeniable signs to foreign eyes: age, sex, fertile or not fertile? Pubescent, it has made me unapproachable, in the kingdom of men I am the filth, on the women's chessboard, the waiting pawn hidden behind a haughty queen who alone will choose the moment when to move herself. There, blind and naive I will bump into one of the black knights . . . . For the moment, I am able to split myself: I am a pawn and a player at the same time. Concentration. On myself, things, the street. I am able to sit in my room for hours with a single objective: to twist my spirit. The eyes play a secondary role, thought, the conductor of the operation, occupies the totality of the flat unobstructed field composed of solitude coupled with boredom. I pay attention to each one of my gestures, by indirect concentration, I give them an exaggerated importance: an outstretched arm, one leg crossed over the other, a lifted elbow, a feverish ankle symbolize the first wish of existence, then I inscribe the logic of my synchronized ballet on a little imaginary blackboard. The next day I joyfully perform my choreography, often with the purpose of improving it, but with my gestures resembling those of yesterday; at the end of the day, I have the lousy feeling of monotony in my throat. I orbit myself like the earth around the sun, a fly hungry for adventure. A useless round that makes of the mind the epicenter of the body, the body the epicenter of the mind. And a mouse locked up in a cage bites its own tail.

Sometimes I find myself thinking of Ourdhia. Whenever I remove myself from the planet of the Ego, my consciousness, certainly, enjoys distracting itself with that of others, yet another clumsy dialogue between the absurd and the absurd, but the emptiness sometimes fills itself with strange figures rendered real by words, alive by sheer force of will. Memory suddenly rears up in my room, rips me away from time, catapults me toward foreign summits, and like an only slightly daring adventuress I hang out on a particular peak of the past with the essence of an already lived adventure in my flask. No special persuasion and no trickery either, just a face flashing out of a far off present time. It's not out of kindness that I resuscitate the past, but simple desire for eternity; Ourdhia is a mythical heroine, dead and buried but more available than the living. With no emotion, I embrace her body and the countryside to which it belongs. No tears. No regrets. My heart is a blank tablet scrubbed down by indifference, smeared with gel, carved in rock where feeling cannot easily persist.

Solitude has taught me coldness, selfishness and resignation. I don't know how to cry for others anymore. I've simply forgotten. I've misplaced the instructions for the correct function of the tear machine. Head heavy and mouth dry, I force myself in vain, nothing comes, except for a grimace in the mirror which makes me barely able to smile. And what good would it do if I could remember? My tears would only hear the echo of identical tears spaced out by the play of the walls and the restricted horizon. I am my own echo, my own interlocutor, my own sadness!

My house is the temple of austerity. Tenderness, joy, or pity are scalped by my father's grand inquisitor gaze and my mother's hate. The rare bursts of laughter or despair quickly join the daily clutter behind a piece of furniture; there between the wood and the plaster our attempts to feel emotion lie dying. I wouldn't dream of mentioning love. Insane invention, miasma imported from the West, lying illusion, youth's perversion. At our home, no luck, no excitement, no meeting. This displaced emotion whose value tapers off the more one ages, is annihilated by calculation, friendly arrangement and interest. Your "love" curve is traced; quite impossible to drift away from it, it cuts off access to any influence that would distance it from its finality. Everything is ready. Suffice it to choose the propitious moment. Who's talking about destiny?

As for desire . . . for some it gets painfully satisfied on the tile floor of a "blind alley" of a kitchen, while others make do with the night and an experienced hand under experienced covers!

I invent deadly illnesses for myself, burning lungs, a muddled brain, pitted intestines and biliary nausea but my mother never lets herself be tricked. With her legendary delicateness she sticks a disgusting herbal tea into my mouth and I've had it for the evening! Invaded by the thorn of a baobab tree in a state of accelerated growth, smothered by a swarm of bumble bees and floored by the effluvia of a rotten throat, I let myself die in the bottom of my bed, my only companion the shadow of my mother imprisoned between my arms, stirring up the emptiness.

And I fall asleep, my head cornered between two tuberous breasts, hoping that tomorrow will really be tomorrow.

Today: a lesson about things or how not to be bored in a Moslem country when one is a Moslem girl.

God has pointed his accusing index finger at my forehead, I musn't go out, must avoid my father's look when I'm having my period, live hidden like a thing in the shadow of my mother, accept whippings, and persuade myself that I have been naughty. Abdication of the senses, of revolt and rebellion.

Triumph of resignation, of passivity and of fear. Child of a mute but hardly deaf male who sired me, of a female disguised as a eunuch who gives birth, sister of two vegetable monsters about to die, I have no means of help, my mother is preparing her revenge behind my back, it is through me, the only fertile one in the house, that she avenges her birth, our existence and her sex; in the caldron of her being she has concealed the mixture for her next ambush, stupid mother, the smell of hate floats all the way up to my room.

How not to be bored in a Moslem country when one is a Moslem girl?

First of all, know nothing of time, it doesn't pass, it passes away, hide clocks and watches, hourglasses and metronomes, appointment books and calendars; take into consideration things and only things while forgetting that on the other side of the ocean teenagers walk hand in hand without a God or a father to block their way; then cultivate the imagination that will deport you to another time in the shadow of a fertile tree, creation itself; if that doesn't work, then take refuge in the street, looking down from your window on high, but there, if your words don't sustain you, you'll ram into the horror of a very unseductive reality.

End of the intermission.

I do my room, undo it, do it over, undo it again. Stool to the right, bed in the middle, desk in front of the window, pillows on the floor, lights out, faucets on, faucets off, door closed, curtains pulled, dark, light, rectangular, round, curved, my insurgency through the most extraordinary forms, stool on bed, bed on desk, chair in sink, and lampshade on ceiling. Hysterical architecture, projection of my thoughts onto things. It's not only the monotony of time that you have to shorten but also the monotony of space! The setting has an effect on my biological rhythm, on my moods; an open window makes me hungry, an undone bed makes me want to sleep, a light turned on in full daylight makes me want to flee. I enervate my senses so they'll fall asleep better, I speed up my carotid tempo all the better to die. Wearied by things and my lack of patience in the face of a slow, disorderly and capricious imagination, I burrow into one of the four corners of my cell and inflict on myself "swirling" pinchmarks, thumb and index finger pressures on a piece of innocent flesh whose only fault is tenderness. My father has been the trigger of my violence, the responsible party whom I hereby accuse.

Secret accomplice of Satan, he has given me a taste for limitless pleasure but I pay dearly the next day. Bruises, aches, scrapes . . . felonious activity or the destruction of self by self.

It was an autumn day. So melancholy when everything is dying without me, I felt lighter however than on the other days. Was this a first instant of happiness? The leaves were disappearing with the passing of the hours, so that the only tree in the little garden was left nude, a bearer of new horizons. My field of sight had enlarged considerably, and joyfully I was lighting a cigarette in front of the entire city.

Always there when I don't expect him, my father was watching me consume my last instants of solitary pleasure when my eyes met his; with a nervous and guilty hand, I chased away the last spiral smoke curls breathed out by my punishable sighs. The pack had been lying around on the dining room table with a provocative air that calls out to sin. How could I resist?

He approached me. Burst out laughing. Surprised at hearing the sound of his joy, I started to smile and gave him a complicitous look. This happy father offered me another cigarette! Embarrassed, I refused but he insisted. Trembling and confused I couldn't light it. He delicately took it from my mouth and lit a match at the end of the little blond tobacco column, turning it into a smoking ember. I thanked him, forgetting that the gestures of my master were never inconsequential. I was waiting for a word. A reproach. Infinitesimal, but a reproach anyway! Nothing came. He handed the cigarette to me, and, on the way, smashed it onto my smile. He drew four little blisters with the red iron, then, one hand glued to the nape of my neck, he pushed harder so as to smash the cigarette against the enamel of my teeth. "You want to smoke. So how's this!" he said, leaving my bedroom.

The burn, lessened by surprise, was hardly perceptible. A smell of grilled meat went from the red skin tissues around my mouth up to my nostrils. I popped the blisters, the lymph of a new story flowed into the fleshy ashtray. It was hot and salty. For the future, a little harelip was born.

A two-headed angel, sitting on the barren tree, laughed derisively at my expense.

Worn out by more of the same, the repetitiveness and emptiness of solitude, my body yields its ballet of energetic but useless gestures to the repose of the senses. So I pull my chair to the window and let my eyes fall on a dirty street animated by scantily dressed wretches, scamps and idle little girls.

My city is an old seductress fallen asleep, her breath slow, her dream audible but winded, she dozes at the edge of the bed of her first loves. Transient lovers, possessive mistresses, jealous husbands, timid suitors and young girls, enamored with Beauty, have covered her body with flowers and kisses, burned incense before her soul out of admiration and respect. Unsubjugated, generous, great courtesan, intoxicated by Life and happiness, fortunate and affectionate lover, she was the symbol of grace at the center of private dinner parties, the rage of the world press; the rapture of men, women and children. Congratulated at formal affairs, effigy of the entire planet, crowned by the gods and goddesses of Antiquity, ministers, queens, kings, princes and princesses, presidents, dukes and baronesses, democrats and dictators have embraced her body; seducing the leading men, getting drunk with the celebrities, she provoked the jealousy of her own kind, the admiration of housewives and the regret of old women ruined by time. Eternal, at each love reborn, imaginative and fertile, she baptized boats, train tracks, saints, and first airplanes, and kept in her breast, jealous but full of foresight, the most beautiful writings dedicated to her beauty. Muse, model, half-sane wisewoman, foster mother, intoxicated lover, she was the cradle of audaciousness, of joy and of glory; writers, poets, painters, sculptors fell asleep in the hollow of her stomach: the famous bay of Algiers. They inspired her finery, engraved her body, colored her surroundings, varnished her silhouette; and her sex, from which flamboyant gardens, fruit trees and rectilinear plantations burst forth, was satisfied by alert and delicate hands that gathered her flowers at the right moment, and always she would be reborn like a delicious and bewitching virgin in the midst of all the lovers greeting her.

Henceforth spinster, wilted by the years, trampled on by new men, she only delivers her secret to those who know how to look. Her stomach gives refuge to visionaries, catacomb open to the public, cosmos of the old world, carries too many children, feeds too many starving. It falls like a pouch pierced by the poacher's sword, thus discharging onto the streets, the sidewalks, the dead ends, and the most beautiful avenues, a pile of moldy entrails building up into mountains of dead lives and dried-out memories. Uneducated children play with the final vestiges of the past in the darkness of the shadows around her eyes, between two worn-out thighs that still spread apart to bless the rotten fruits of the dying motherland; she has folded up her arms against the warriors of the new years, and in her breast dies the tonifying milk of yesteryear's writings. Her poor tubercular chest can no longer hide the painful spectacle of two nipples too often embraced, too ridiculed, and too scorned. Lift your hands browned by old age spots to implore the mercy of gods who have fled for more laughter-filled lands! No more angels, no more women, no more flowers, terraces or laughing echoes, only the faded plans of a vast prison which betray the blood of martyrs. Veil among veils, sinner among sinners, the rotting among the rotten, is it the payoff for too long a happiness or the ravages of Atlas mountain crows? And her sex, devastated by very solitary hands, waves a sad handkerchief in the distance: the flag of surrender!

Her moldings, ornaments from before the war*, superficial brooches on a stone dress, stayed with her. Faithfully. Last party adornments forgotten because tenacious, devastated by gnawing filth, they resemble blistered scars, memories of a clumsy operation carried out by a clumsy doctor beneath the eyes of clumsy students in a climate of clumsiness; her parks, where women and children once cooed under padded umbrellas, are yellow mops, moth-eaten by dehydration, over-crowded by nostalgic men and lunatics in search of a bed. No more elevators, no

---

*war: The "war" refers to the Algerian war of independence, between Algeria and France, 1954-1962. Algeria gained its independence in 1962.

more canopies, no more shop windows to charm the curious, just sheets hanging between the polluted air and walls dirtier than the sleeping homeless and the medieval street merchants who frighten me.

The dogs eat the garbage, the rats eat the cats and the dogs are bitten by the garbage rats, so, like that, the only animals of the illogical ecosystem, the rats, linked to men, participate in the massacre of the city. The children fall asleep in sheets pitted like their mother's sex, the elevators stuck at the bottom of gaping open columns refuse out of disgust to go up, urine embalms each stair step with its ammonia, each landing, the odors of old sheep escape from bloody butcher shops, quartered sections of meat ooze, butcher hooks often short of meat display exhausted skeletons instead, sawdust imprisons the emphysema-stricken flies, the sewers burst, prices skyrocket, slums contaminate the heart of the city, malignant tumors, the shanties, buckled by the sickly blood cells of their inhabitants, clutch the walls of the poverty-stricken neighborhoods, little girls equipped with plastic blue pails drink the water from the gutter, the choleric water, men piss on the trees, children play under the trees, rats gnaw the trees, the pavements stink, cars hum on the asphalt, the August sun burns the alleys, old men blow their noses in their fingers, the Saracen women weep solitude and boredom, alcohol and dominoes kill boredom, the sexes are bored to death, spirits melt, bodies merge, at seven o'clock the masculine mass moves toward the main alleys, the town heights are reserved for grand properties, the air up there is fresher, the Mozabite says "That's what's missing!," glass is piled up on top of the walls of the properties, boys fight each other with razor blades, mothers marry off their daughters, a white veil passes again and again in front of our house, the mosques scream despair, hanging on the foreign high school fences young men masturbate in front of young girls running toward their future, time has stopped from the moment of our first cries, acid in hand the brown beards[1] throw vitriol on uncovered girls, sadness is inscribed on the face of wandering children, on the slab of the monument to the dead lifted toward the sky like a phallus toward its mistress, the veil is exchanged for a dark dress with overlong sleeves, my sisters cover their ankles and repudiate their sex, carried by divine truth the believers go forth into the city like conquerors of the new era, rats eat cats and bite children, night roars, day gives way to despair, thighs bleed, fathers whip their daughters, others expiate their sinful birth on stinking sidewalks, on their knees, down on the ground, marriages are bloody, the derbouka* resonates, solitude is at the bottom of my cup, poison poisons, fetuses fall from the window, hyenas cry out, brothers embrace, the billhook cuts, the star moves in procession, Zohr binds her breasts, objects scoff at me, the city moves closer to the desert, my father rapes Ourdhia, the knife cuts away my vulva, I am afraid.

And the old women roll themselves up in flowered dresses as protection against the plague.

---

[1]The term "brown beards" (*barbes brunes*) refers to the usually bearded male fundamentalist Moslems.
*Debouka: a kind of drum

III

This afternoon my mother is receiving her foster sister: Aunt Khadidja. Excited by the arrival of new gossip, she whirls around the living room with a lightness I didn't know she had, a smile is suspended on her lips for the rest of the day, her henna-reddened braid flies from right to left and sometimes rests on a drooping breast like a snake halting on a crumbling mound, her comings and goings in the suddenly laughter-filled house make her seem like a mischievous child, she airs out her thighs by constantly lifting up her house dress which she then knots and tucks between her stomach and her thighs. No, I'm not dreaming, my mother seems happy! She clacks her gilded slippers while singing an old refrain by Farid el Atrhach, impassive Zohr helps her remove the chairs, roll a small carpet, move the couch and arrange a bouquet of crepe paper flowers, cookies in the shape of gazelle horns pile up in floury mountains, oil from the cakes oozes into soup plates like lava from a rancid butter volcano and doughnuts suffocate under low grade sugar. My mother's hands rummage about in a jewelry box, Leyla has taken refuge behind the couch, and I hear her crunching on pieces of burned dough.

Someone rings at the door. The celebration begins. There's no doubt about it, a new plot is being hatched, even the front door bell doesn't have its usual sound, the ringer's more pleasing, more joyful too. Zohr, the sickly plant, fluffs up the couch cushions for a last time, my mother plants a hair pin in the nape of her red neck and runs in the direction of the entryway. I recognize the voice of Aunt K. in a piercing ululation, immediately we lift the living room door from its hinges so our fat aunt can get in.

After the never-ending polite greetings, the kisses that rend the air, my aunt, my blissful aunt, makes her way toward us. The rowboat goes in sideways in the little hallway, a violent puffing accompanies each of her difficult movements, I recognize in the winded little kisses the odor of a foreign perfume, and anxious to reach the couch she accelerates the pace. Rime, her daughter, and therefore my cousin, somehow or other supports her in her grotesque walk. Rime is fifteen and still possesses the grace of adolescence, making one momentarily forget that she'll be like her mother one day with her slightly drooping thick lower lip and stretched out eyes, this rather rounded Moorish woman could have some charm if an incipient goiter didn't give her the air of an ox in heat.

Aunt K., wife of Mister Z., nursed from the same breast as my mother; her husband, a shady little civil servant, made a fortune thanks to illicit trafficking in foreign currencies; it is for this reason that our aunt seems "evolved" as my mother says, a little envious and admiring. Always back and forth between Paris and Algiers to have her hair done and pick up a few purchases, Aunt K. graciously comes and sees us once a year to bring back a little souvenir. Last year it was camemberts, perfumed soaps and a hairdryer, today it's camomile shampoo with a young naked girl on the packaging, chocolates, an electric train for Leyla and a muslin cloth as light as air which I will use to dab my wounds.

Aunt K. drops onto the couch, its springs suddenly stretched to death, squealing in pain; out of breath, she fans her face with a flowered scarf, throws her veil behind the couch (it falls on Leyla's head: in broad daylight, darkness!) then hikes her dress up to her thighs. The oozing flesh proudly spreads out on the cushions, a black stocking tries desperately to hold back the padded skin but the devastating fat makes a hole in the fabric netting in order to breathe! A brown head of hair bounces onto her back, immeasurably long nails lengthen her fleshy blood-sausage fingers congested by overly shiny rings, a mass of paint dries on her eye-lashes and sometimes falls as navy blue powder on the badly drawn line of dark kohl. Greasy lipstick encircles her pussy-shaped mouth and edges into nostrils so gaping that one can see a tapestry of stiff hairs rise up in the dark caverns. Her body? A down comforter you could almost melt into, so velvety and com-fortable its texture, but looking closer you quickly lose the ur-gency! In fact, exploded veins draw little rivers of dried blood on her skin, making me suddenly want to vomit. She is wearing a black linen dress, the neckline buttons have popped, leaving be-hind a little thread and a gaping button hole.

Zohr has placed a little radio near us. Through the silvery speaker the Asmahan choirs exhale words with sugary intona-tion as sticky as the grain of the tâmina*. Aunt K., suddenly over-taken by romantic feeling in sharp contrast with her body, throws back her head of hair and closes her eyes as if we no longer ex-isted; in turn my mother lets herself go, and I hear her say with a voice cracked by regret: "Ah yes!," the little sentence penetrates our souls, its exclamation point wraps around our hearts and she wavers between sadness and surprise. Tick tock tick tock goes the metronome of our guts. Stupidly, without really knowing what's happening, we the ignorant offspring echo back: "Ah yes!"

The two of them united by memories whose exact details I will never know, the pride of their secret appears on their faces, palms spread out and bodies numbed by an ecstasy newly birthed in the depth of time: the sunrise of their adolescence.

The beach of memories, brand new, shiny, stretches and stretches inside the house bringing with it new houses, new char-acters under a new sun. The city is quite far away. My father too. A young man's look, a glance at a closed shade, a hand behind the curtains and behind so much more, the story is woven of an

---

Tâmina: semolina cake

57

imaginary love in a dark room, but at the seashore. It was to the East of Algiers. Mouloud's firecrackers, the meat left over from the celebration, my unknown grandmother's endless stories and her famous breakfast dumplings. Always this man in a white sweater and the fishermen whistling at night, a hand in the water to attract the morays. The song of the fishermen. Yes, I hear it now. In the distance, on the beach off-limits to respectable girls. Under the verandah, two crickets chirp at the night, the maid bathes in the laundry basin; old and worn out, she grabs her two breasts in her fists crying out "My rags! look at my rags!," the celebration, the little brother becomes a man, there is blood on his robe and henna under his feet, the evening coolness of the interior courtyard, the women still have not finished speaking of and getting closer to their death. Uncle Sam has fallen in love with a Djinnia* and the little devils waltz under the eyelids of little girls fallen asleep to the East of Algiers.

We meditate on our mother's past as one meditates on a nameless faceless tomb but with grandiose silence and respect because it is dead and the memorial stone says clearly that it is dead. The tomb spits it out, its death, it undresses it and exhibits it with a conspicuous stone so we do not walk on it and its downy covering of weeds, clearly showing that there is nothing left. Just a face without a name or a name without a face, what's the difference!

We imagine, we soil the memory of the dead; after all, the past doesn't belong to us, but it's good to gather our thoughts, we have more respect than we need, again faith returns, solemnity takes over our faces and our names, and the dead jostle each other between the words and the images. Stop thinking about it! Everything is over. A tear flows under my aunt's make-up, the little salt snake furrows between the pores and the cream so as to open up a passage, my mother knits her brow, but nothing comes, just an image blurred by the others. This is called remorse.

Tâmina: semolina cake

I hear little girls giggling under their blankets. They don't know yet. Like Leyla. Too bad. They're locked inside, but at the seashore! The two women are pushing the truth. It's not important. Later, I'll also invent for myself furtive loves, beautiful delicate males will throw stones at my window, beautiful faces on beautiful names; I will recount to my little ones the warmth of their unknown grandfather, their grandmother's tenderness; in my turn I will lie in order to fill in the empty gaps of my adolescence; I was living before You, before this sordid house, before your cruel father! And they will feel guilty. As I do today. Guilty for being bored, for hating their parents, guilty for holding a grudge against the men in the street, these men who trouble their sleep, guilty for exposing their flesh, cut so they can find a touch of pleasure, an underlying mystery in this reasonless existence, whereas happiness is so close by, just over there, in a dark room, at the seashore, east of Algiers!

One arranges one's past as well as one can, especially when one is a woman in a Moslem country. Oh yes! They were ashamed to have been locked up, ashamed of their tears, of the frustration, ashamed of their dreams! Aunt K. simulated a hint of modernity underneath her veil, but when she went out into the street, her veil remained, like a burden on her shoulders, and she had imposed it on Rime for her own good. The beach is off limits for girls with self-respect. They only had the right to the smell of algae coming through the shutters, to the noise, at night, of motor boats leaving the port and of the water against the sea wall; this, poor mothers, this is what I do to your memories! Isn't it your own mothers who married you to two city men passing through, in order to tear you away from your little miserable life, from the room situated at the seashore, but closed? Your erasable memories don't interest me, they are as false as mine will be. I hold a grudge against you for having reconstituted all for your daughters, right there, and not one detail has escaped you! You knew however. You knew the pain of being locked up waiting. Why start again? From mother to daughter sadness is a "jewel" which one can't do without any longer, an inheritance, a congenital illness, transmissible and incurable! Murderous mothers!

After having purged themselves in the yellow field of the past, the monsters find reality again with surprising ease. Aunt K. wipes her face with a paper napkin, a few pieces of fluff staying stuck to her pock-marked skin, my mother grabs hold of the teapot, pours the burning liquid into a multicolored glass; once the glass is filled, she opens the lid and pours the liquid into another container. She starts the operation over seven times: this number brings luck. Luck for what in fact?

Not one drop escapes from the containers, just the steam which reddens her face already discolored by the past. Aunt K. looks at her, breathes with pleasure in front of the greasy cakes then calms her palate with two muscat grapes. Her voluminous thighs taking up the whole sofa require my cousin Rime to stay on the armrest, she smiles stupidly and seems to prefer her bench-like seat to a pouf cushion, soft and inviting, but situated too far away from her "mommy!"

The tea is served. Aunt K. adds three spoonfuls of liquid honey and loudly inhales the hot mint while blinking her eyes; she rests her glass, lets loose a burp, and with neither fear nor remorse rubs her hands and observes us. She finds that Zohr has again lost weight, scolds her for her ribs, her too conspicuous veins, her winged back and her trembling knees. You'll never find a husband, Zohr! Old maid! that's what you are, an indecent old maid! how can one let oneself waste away like that? Who will want you my poor child with your eyes circled in black and your skeletal hands? Zohr says nothing, she contents herself with a smile then closes her left fist to hide an invisible ring: her wedding ring with Death. My turn. Compliments burst out with a skill that doesn't inspire confidence in me. They spread here and there in the room, bang against the walls, rebound on the couch and roll under my aunt's tongue. My mother is proud. Not me. Look at this beautiful hair and these eyes so big for such a delicate body! How discrete! The spitting image of her father! I resemble him, it's true, always silent, I listen, I observe. We have two ears, two eyes but a single mouth. That's how I explained my muteness to my fat aunt. My sad air? comes from the family. Apparently with me it's an added charm. My delighted mother winks none too discretely at my Aunt K. who immediately winks back.

I see you. I feel the plot. The way she wiggles around on her armrest with a little smile at the corner of her mouth which emphasizes her glistening cheek, Rime seems to be in on the intrigue; Zohr looks at me with compassion and the objects around me take on life: trembling with fear the light blinks, the pouf cushions move away from me, the living room mirror splits, the door of the little garden bangs, a car starts up, and my mother's grape-mauve teeth give her the raspy voice of a cinnamon peeler. I feel even more alone among these blissful apathetic women. Alone in the crowd, disrespectful toward the group and the family, misanthrope on the edge of death, what could they understand of my sadness? I live it alone, I push it along like a burden and sometimes it even keeps me warm. Too late today to separate myself from it.

My aunt's thighs, Rime's fetid breath, all these breasts wobbling with the disgrace of monsters nauseate me. And now, set against me, the weight of the secret, the intrigue. A piercing and sporadic acid surge lifts up my ribs, congests my skin and blackens my lips. Dark, closed, my mouth resembles a tulip whose mucous petals barely hold back the words of fury. I must leave before it's too late. Taking advantage of a resounding burst of laughter, I get up, steal away through the hall, and disappear behind the walls. No one will really notice my absence, Zohr maybe . . . . and again, so taken with the bride (the illness), far from us she flirts with Death and her smiles are addressed only to the cunning one that she carries on her back.

I go up to my room. The objects scoff at me. The oversized window proudly boasts an impenetrable clarity. Behind the glass: life. Far away. It is mocking. Violence goes up my spine to reach my most sensitive nerves; hate syringe, cup filled with blows, soured mouth, clenched fists, here is my beautiful body dear mother, here is my soul! And the foam froths at the corners of my lips.

With betrayal of the senses, unnamable, I reverse myself into another me: decadence. I lamentably rip apart a yellow foam pillow, fly, fly, fly, the little cotton wadding pillows! I knock over my night lamp, the desk, rip the mattress from the box mattress and hammer its innocent springs with my anger, I trample on the lampshade, and its white stays, detached from their axis, and standing up against me now, wound my ankles. Until they bleed. Oh blood! I wipe my walls with the bedspread, then paint them gaudily with tincture of iodine: Partitions of my exile, how beautiful you are all made up like that! I bang my left temple against my window handle, the iron echoes in my head but it's not enough, the opening laughs even more derisively. Relic of solitude, frame of emptiness, emblem of imprisonment and frustration, filthy liar! Your window pane tricked me, it doesn't contain sun, or air, or the shadows that pass over me when I approach you.

I make my room into a mortuary cell where the mixed bloods, the upside down senses, and the most abject maxims deafen walls and pillows, head and body. The women's laughter comes up the staircase, grabs onto the handrail and waits behind my door. I am depleted. Wait, wait, always wait! I plunge my fist into the now fully blossomed tulip and rip off the bud which prevented me from speaking, then I lean my head against the bars of an overturned chair, and in a tone unknown to me I say: "I love you,

Daddy, squeeze my icy hand and breathe in the perfume of the bleeding tulip."

A crimson colored thin line has descended from my gums and dried on my gaping throat.

My knee is very badly scraped. The foot of the lamp is broken. A piece of ceramic has made its way into the intricate nervous pathways of my knee joint; a purple snake is coming out of its lair; awakened from too long a sleep, it stretches itself gracefully all along my leg; delicate layer of fresh varnish or little blood worm, it runs over my skin at will and takes off only to disappear behind my calf; reaching my heel, it squishes into large drops onto the tile flooring and I hear myself murmur: Reddish scales, embryonic rose petals, thinned-out strawberry leaves, make my prison tiles joyful! Little macabre symphony for hidden celebration of unbalanced senses.

I hear the front door close on Aunt K., the house lightens up, my ankle resembles a bicolor stained glass window, the small veins form strange figurines, an exploded coral, a crazed underwater plant, lost, insane; the veins intersect, uncross, become entangled, they try to impress me! I've knocked the machine out of gear, beneath my skin insane stalks blister like tar in the August sun. My tongue licks the paving; agile, it runs over the already dry drops, I apply myself like a puppy discovering a new toy. Thanks to a skillful contortion of my chest and head, I inhale this liquid which flows only in me hoping to please my dispossessed veins.

My window shutters bang, a distant spiraling murmur comes up from the street, infiltrates my room and makes all of the objects waltz. Tornado of cries and noises. Impatient cars shriek through their horns. A bus stops near our house. Exhales. Its doors hesitate before opening. The smelly rubber tires make the walls of my house tremble. A shiver disappears into the rings of my spine. I do a job on myself imagining the worst. Another little girl must have been run over. Her arms crossed, her skirt lifted, she was groaning beneath the iron machinery so much heavier than her mother's stomach. The passengers wanted to get off in order to lighten up the vehicle but the doors, stuck by fear and guilt, stayed closed. So, they pounded on the window panes. Dazed by the noise and the wine of death I clumsily get up again. My body stumbles against the suddenly black space. Two eyes. Two eyes that look like ink bubbles attached to glossy paper occupy my room. Dark. My father is standing in the frame of the door that I had forgotten to lock. For how long had he been there watching me dance on the tile floor bubbling with blood? A little girl is imprisoned in the asphalt. Did he know? I stand bent forward. Under the iron, the horizon no longer exists. The din grows. The sky catches fire, the terraces of the Atlas mountains crumble and roll desert stones down onto the capital square. A vulture perched on an antenna balances itself between emptiness and emptiness. There is blood under the window panes and on my ankles. Child's blood. A dark countryside thins out under her eyes, rusted pipes, air vents, gas tank openings. Death forces her to look. It is burning hot. Her cheeks are coated with tar. Beyond, well beyond the tires, a foot runs by. A shoe has fallen in our little garden. A child's sandal. My father still looks at me. Did he know? The bus doors finally open, the passengers murmur in the crime street.

The body is little and frail. Finally, they figure it out! She took off after a ball, the bus was running late. Without seeing each other they crossed each other's path, without getting to know each other they intertwined. A siren sweeps the field crowded with idlers. I move aside. The bus maneuvers as best it can. Let us avoid squashing the soul! At the edge of the sidewalk, a toy in hand, her little friend waits for her to be pulled from the iron wreckage. No air left to live. It's time to leave. A man cries. I approach my father. He is breathing. Above the city. My head is glued against his legs, his robe smells good of cologne water. From his slow breath, no emotion shows through. The hourglass empties and fills with blood. He counts his rose stone rosary beads. The minute was long for her too. The bus takes off. A bit of scalp with a braid turns in the engine.

For now everything is calm. He and I are alone. And still many things separate us: law, religion, our sexes, and our hate. A thin line of light transports the ghost of the little girl who plays with the fringes of the lampshade above my room. I would like to sleep on a bench, hide myself in a little steep street, I would like to swim under the sun, run in the city, piss in the stairwells, and fight like a street urchin, I would like to eat with the Mozabites, flirt with the bus driver, drink coffee in a cafe and tear the Saracen women's veils, I would like to lie down at the foot of the martyr's statue, engrave my name on the Saint's tile and die in the shadow of the Tenere tree, I would like to melt into the noises of the street, look men in the eyes, tease the rats and feed the insane, I would like to be a building, a sacred tile, a tomb stone, a trampled down flower. Is that liberty then, Daddy?

He was on my mother's body and he was crying. He drove himself to distraction wailing his pain, and I was watching!

The male amongst females the best he'll ever do is engender three bodies with gaping sex. Shame on him! Where's he going to hide all day long? He saw me being born. He saw me naked. And he still kept crying. Nevertheless I had his eyes. He cried with his head in his hands, a wild rat under his belly. He backed off from the sorry spectacle, the ground gave out under him, the gods were punishing him. One more time. Poor Daddy! In the street the neighbors point at him, the plane trees shriek with laughter, the walls snicker, the family pokes fun, little girls die from carelessness and the men embrace each other to console themselves. The tolling resounds, the sick animal prowls in search of a shelter but his kingdom is not mine. I hold my arms out toward him, nothing moves under his woman's dress. Rigged with a penis he has to prove something. To always be proving. Before, he had no moustache, just some hardly visible pale black down. Now, with pride the dense curls rise above the mute slit to make the difference unmistakable!

Tapering fingers, manicured nails, hairless muscles and slightly aquiline nose, the male-female stood at the doorstep of the forbidden door as the women bled. Outside, the little girl was at the point of death. Inside, I was opening my veins and summoning pleasure. Solitary, indecent but well deserved. The onlookers had stopped walking, the cars had stopped moving, wallowing in "happiness" I licked the satanic liquid, thus defying religious rule, forgetting the oppressive presence of my father in these walls of boredom. Smashed by the engine, she sighed for a last time and night arrived in full afternoon. Sweeping the August sun she carried in a black curtain the anguish of children and the regrets of negligent mothers. Chance? Coincidence? Misfortune? I was climaxing while the little girl was slipping into sleep. The line of the past cut the line of the present at a coarse point: the full stop of death.

My father still doesn't move. Me, I look like a prior. I want to feel his fingers running through my locks, his nails against my skull, I want him to undo my hair then redo it all wrong, I want the mark of his fingers on my forehead and his knee bone in my stomach. Like a cat drunk on *eau de cologne*, I screw up my eyes and give him a few affectionate nods with my head. Nothing. Not a word. Not a gesture. A child has been put into the drawer in a morgue. I want to feel his body against my body, see his shoulders bend down to bless the fruit of his efforts. School has been closed for a long time. Somebody is missing at the table. I want to discover his woman's body. The white is blinding. It isn't for this reason that my eyelashes have fallen out. Discover the delicate shapes with my skin, my veins and my heart. No ties possible except for two thighs squeezed too tight. The sound of breathing burdened by hate takes over my whole room. I was going to pay. Tomorrow. He's not the one who'll punish me. He's too disgusted to move. Another man will handle it for him. I smiled. He saw me smile. Supreme insult in this house where joy is forbidden. I cried out, I licked, I loved a body that came out of my body, an escaped sense! His friend, sitting on a bit of broken sidewalk, was repairing a broken doll. I kiss his indoor sandals. The leather is strong. It is spread out in several little straps, cut short by a large buckle. The silver spine scratches my chin. Reaching the ankles, I bury my head beneath the robe which resembles a wedding sheet not yet used. I go up in the elevator of the senses. Accompanied by fear I was pursuing this strange path of emotion when a violent blow from his knee made me stumble backwards. In a burst of diabolical laughter I was spread out shamelessly on my hateful decadence. The blood had long since dried up; imprisoned by the furrows, framing my prison tiles in red. The door that closed behind him again symbolically closes my old hopes. Now I know. I know that he will never give me this pleasure I painfully invent in my voluntary mutilations. I wasn't asking for anything major: a kiss, a caress, a smile . . . . I'd even have been happy with a sigh.

No. He preferred leaving me to solitude. The dreadful solitude that makes the weakest want to die.

He was the only man in the house, and with strange ease I was forgetting my blood ties, turning my very own engenderer, him of the indiscrete eyes, into an object of lust, and the primary cause of each of our illnesses.

The cry from a neighboring street dies out, a draft makes the front door bang, the only tree in the small garden reaches out with its main branch, the gate opens halfway: a little girl clutches the wrought iron bars.

In the bottom of a cold drawer a child was waiting for someone to come and fetch her.

∽IV∽

I take a chance and open my shutter, the glare is on my side so that no one would risk going blind for a lousy look. Drunk on air, dizzy from the sun, I hang on to the guardrail of the windowsill so as not to lose my balance on the tile floor; rent in pieces by luminous beams I'm like a foreign saint preparing to pronounce the last commandment. Ruler of Moorish women, spokeswoman of silence, mistress of Men and of things, the street, the city, the world belongs to me. I am the main artery of the event, the prime mover of beings, the female liberator of yesteryear's citadels, Cassandra of the new century. I determine the perspective, hold up the horizon; nothing escapes my view through luminous slits in the chestnut shutters, the receptive supports of my emotions.

An intolerably long car pulls me from my dreaming. The exhaust pipe spits out its stinking breath for a last time and dies in a terrifying rasp, taking by surprise the two young men sitting not too far away. The burning tires, cooling off now, tough it out under the sun, their hubcaps shine like silvery spheres from another planet far beyond the moon. What is this machine of unhappiness doing under my window, in my street, smack in the middle of slums and garbage? Who gives himself the right to come and bury us even further in our gray sadness under the sun? Who dares trouble our impoverished and idle children?

The gleaming machinery distinguishes itself from the sidewalks and the asphalt color with a proud air, it accentuates the age and unreliability of the other cars. The street is calm, a few murmurs animate the plane trees, the curtains across the street move, and an old maidservant beats the blankets with a stick to rid them of dreams and sins fermenting under them since the night before.

In the distance I hear the trolley reach the center of town, a black monster has disturbed the street's usual character, the men's boldness, the children's rest, a thousand pairs of eyes popping out of their heads travel through the air to watch the beautiful car make a display of herself, the gleaming insect unfolds one of her wings, an "encapped" man laboriously gets out of the dark vehicle. We all secretly think that it's probably the chauffeur. Standing between a garbage can and a smelly gutter, he smooths out his wrinkled suit, stretches his arms toward the sky as if to implore God's mercy, the curve of his back, his wrinkled pants pleat, the two damp spheres across his work jacket show just how difficult the trip through misery was. A little boy, ecstatic because of the curious presence of the long-limbed "scrap metal," approaches the radiator, the chauffeur looks at him with amusement while inspecting the front of the car with a dustcloth-hand-kerchief; the task finished, he catches the little guy by the arm and makes his head swim with questions whispered so low that I have trouble hearing what plot is being hatched beneath my window. After a lot of beating around the bush, the little boy scratches his head, and with a traitorous finger, designates my room. Satisfied, the chauffeur slips a coin into the hip pocket of his pants and gently pushes him away from the car.

My room shines in the street, I am suspended on a solid gold throne, the attention of an entire people, eager to know what is going on, is directed at me. Embarrassed by this new attention lavished on me without even asking my opinion, I grab on tighter to the railing, all the while enduring the chauffeur-laugher's look. I'm not sure, but I believe I see a masculine silhouette in the back seat, encircled by a halo of blue smoke. Yes, there is someone, the chauffeur gets back into his driver's cab and I see him turn distinctly toward the smoky ghost. For a last time he looks at my room, then roars his working tool. The black goddess slowly leaves my street, from the back window ledge two huge eyes shoot an arrow straight into my heart. Instinctively, stupidly I scream: "It's too soon!"

The men under the plane trees, enchanted to finally see my face, sneeringly laugh with excitement. I give them the finger. The incident is closed. My curtains too.

The next day, the day after that, and then again the next day welcomed the same masquerade. Men from neighboring streets had come for the express purpose of attending voyeur-woman's final moments; it's said that a transportation company had organized a special excursion to allow the peasant men to get in on the adventure. The maids were waiting under the sheltering sun protected by parasols set up for the occasion, the children completely occupied the sidewalks, the stairwells, the bus stops, some had made themselves little parade stools, others even ventured into the Aouz Bek garden; a human tide occupied the once silent street and worriedly the other girls watched the tragic little end of their companion. Late at night cars were arrayed in front of the strategic spot, any sham or outrage was fair play in obtaining entrée to the final scene, the slash of the cleaver fatal to Fikria. Beneath her window, a swarm of insects buzzed in expectation of the story's honey, the sap of the adventure. The car would arrive at the twelve strokes of noon, the chauffeur would get out and, hero for a day, start his little tour again, quite familiar now to the inhabitants of "Phantasm Street." He had made himself some friends, even the red-faced grocer deigned to get off his stool and serve him a cup of coffee or discuss the deal, only too happy to speak to the privileged accomplice of the story's author. The owner never got out of his car.

Fikria just wanted to see his face but the man knew that one should never deviate from the path of destiny. Remain faithful to tradition. That's how it was, what must happen will happen, the whole thing was to choose the propitious moment, the most perfect time. With wicked pleasure he prolonged the young girl's anxiety by staying crouched behind the tinted windows of his car: his iron mask!

The horns and the low voices warned her of the danger but the female in love with air and light continued to waltz between a dream and the narrow window opening, a fragment of liberty which she breathed in until out of breath; she clutched the poor guardrail which tried desperately to wound her fingers so she would back up but Fikria never felt pain on account of things; all during her childhood she had cultivated in her garden the flower of observation, and by a curious osmosis ratified by blood pact she herself became object, thing, material. Fikria, the intellectual Moorish woman, amused herself by spying without being seen, and yet for months she was not aware that a terrible plot was being hatched right under her room: She was going to become a woman. A woman under the body of a man.

It's been a week since I holed up in my room. I've pulled the curtains, put my desk against the small glass window; I've clamped shut the window's beak by wrapping its handle with a *serendipitous* string pulled from the center of my blanket; I've stuffed the shutter slots to smother the cries from the supplicating street, oh yeah, I've let it all go, my God, does that shock you? Caught in my own trap, my grip on the events of my street has been exquisite at other times, but today, impious misunderstood female, I'm entangled in the net of a terrifying enterprise. At the twelve strokes of noon, the chauffeur roars his engine, the din grows, the sidewalks applaud, and the executioner burns my last instants of liberty by lighting his little tobacco columns with the strike of a match, and the minutes go up in smoke. I am done. Nude, I stroll about my den with — my only companion — the putrid miasma of my half-dead entrails and the tormented look of my female swimmer. I slice the air with a straightened hanger, its bent body turned into a shameful whip, and order it to start whipping, rapidly, abruptly yet ineffectively. Even with that, I still don't feel anything. My mother does not come to see me, my father has momentarily disappeared from circulation in order to cash in on my destiny, my sisters, faithful in their assigned roles, no longer think about anything but their survival. At night I hear the female that bore me digging around in the cupboard, in her jewelry box, and in her idea box; henceforth she places my lunch at the door of my room, and I wait until she's far away before I open it. Speaking is not allowed. I still retain the benefit of the doubt.

I look around me, the horizon is cut off, space, robbed of its breadth, only sends me back a distressing yet familiar image, and seeing a silhouette blurred by an always uncertain mind, always in search of I don't know what phantasm, I recognize in effect the half-colored picture of my body at the point of death. And in a sudden twist my gaze reflexively takes a curious initiative and throws the tragic but hardly new picture of my useless existence right in my face, leading me straight to an unfathomable countryside : my demise.

Yes, Death was right there. Taking advantage of my inattentive state or perhaps of my extreme attention, it had slid under my door, leaving Zohr momentarily and giving her one night's respite: a night fatal to Fikria . . . . Sitting on the edge of my bed, bony fleshless elbows lifted up, the scythe between her legs, her bald head and sharp skull, her eyes circled in black and her sex gone, Death proposed a genuinely monstrous dilemma. It was he, the faceless man in the car, or She. Her or him? Him or Her!

I was thinking. Her, I knew Her face and Her intentions, she had lived in the house for a long time, acted on the sly with my sister and I already knew Her odor well! What else to say, except that she would not carry me away unjustly, but that she would advance my time just a little. She was messing up the action of the clock face by driving the second hands nuts, that's all!

And so then it was that, unconscious, I grabbed hold of the bent coathanger. If I blew my shot my life would be marked by the seal of sin and my family would be blacklisted until the end of time. Two seconds of hesitation, a couple of swigs of remorse and your "social conventions" can go screw themselves!

I had to calm it down! Calm what? Why, this gaping sex which for months had not stopped growing in order to get ready for a newcomer, a new skin in the form of a cone. Now it was touching the inside of my thighs and weighed heavily in the air when I walked. The little bitch had gotten bigger and a complex mecha-

77

nism had started inside of it, inside of me. Little hairlip, little hereditary abnormality, little traitor, little piece of garbage! Soon it would extend as far as my guts, freed from its sacred inner wall where I couldn't reach even with my longest finger. Yes, it had to be calmed down.

The woman in black helped me lie down on my bed. Straight torso, arms extended, hands ready, my two legs lifted up like arches surrounding the cursed word, enlarged considerably my field of vision, the electric light bulb focused on my pink and striated "inter-course," a lit up triangular form, at once dark and bursting with light, pulpy and anemic, alive and almost dead; I was spreading apart the two little black cushions when, in full light, the peeled sea urchin burdened me with a new emotion: FEAR! It was moving, moaning, begging and one of its dark tears rolled all the way down to my right ankle. Should I, shouldn't I? That was the question! In a hurry, urgent and authoritarian, Death did not leave me time to answer, she inserted in me the icy rod that started a curious voyage through the darkness of my most intimate interior. Immediately, it found the opening. Petrified, I could do nothing to stop it. It was too late. Striking against the soft and rocky structure, grabbing onto my mucous membranes, once in a while sinking into a swamp, it traveled through the pipes and tubes of my machinery without taking into account my groans, half smothered by a complicitous and compassionate pillow.

The iron rod went far up the course of the dried Oued oasis, underbrush, stones, puddles, nothing could stop it in its race against the dark; bent to its liking, it managed to jump the hedges, the holes, the borders and the cushioned peaks; whereupon a sharp pain shook me: the searching head had finally arrived. It poked straight in, stepped back so it could take off, and, my eyes covered but my mind clear, it injected me with such a great pain that I almost tore out my tongue. In spite of a ruby flow which calmed the cruel burning, the iron rod continued higher, and underneath the skin of my belly, I saw it do the snake dance. Like a child discovering a new toy, the little hanger was having fun inside of me, stinging the largest organs to the quick, teasing the littlest ones, going around the longest ones, then, burned by the gears of the working mechanism, it came out glowing from the wound full of blood which didn't stop flowing onto my sheet. I felt like I was getting myself thoroughly drained, everything came out, my mother's hopes, filth, purity, impurity; obsession, my future husband's target, and I sank into a great burst of laughter!

Was I dead or half-conscious? I no longer know. I only remember a dream, a simple dream which took up the whole night.

I was trying to escape it by keeping myself right on the verge of the waking state, my eyes partly open and a hand reaching toward the lightswitch, but it insisted. Weightily. My body then gave into the call of sleep with continual and unpleasant sudden starts, and the dream began, similar to the preceding one.

I was in a clearing burned by the August sun whose edges are ashes and alpha rays, lifted toward the sky, the dry heads of grain prick my calves, the dryness of the level ground distresses me. No surprise, this faded landscape. All around it a dense forest breathes loudly. The song of the bleeding trees calls me, without fear I then abandon the clearing, an odorless place of obvious sterility. And I cry out, "So long, gloomy neutral surface, here I am in the greenhouse of disparate noises, noises of the city, noises of Life!"

I approach the full basin of a fountain whose frost heats up more than an inflaming sun; beneath my impatient step the grasses crunch, scream and grasp each other, I flatten the wastelands and inaugurate the first path among the green tips of the inhuman roots, an unruly tropical creeper wraps around the back of my neck and tells me the story of its rope which frays without ever breaking, the veins of the open trunks beat at the same rhythm as the rapid and unreal growth of an amaranth bouquet, whereas a field of flowers whistles in the wind of the far off hills, their protective petals open up to me and I discover velvet multi-colored buds: a reservoir of sap and of Love. Fresh resin flows perfume the forest and time, slide between the fissures of the muddy little valleys and boil up into my hands, the branches of the plant life enlace each other in a slow and majestic movement, then undulate like the snake who apparently is the son of a blind legless praying mantis. Intoxicated by this overflow of life, I coat my face with ecstasy abundantly secreted by the mobile trees, I roll in the grass, recite bucolic verses and bless nature, wine and pleasure. The transparent stalks massage my body, embrace my face and moisten it with a delicious ambergris perfume, sap runs the length of green limbs and earth's heart drums to accelerate the blood flow of the vegetation's internal organs, the sunflower seeds go round, the cicadas spring, the locusts take wing, the tulips give birth and yellow diamonds decorate the old tree trunks, the gardenias guard, the roses deceive, and a carpet of nasturtiums bursts out of the earth. A colony of ferns joins us and starts a folk dance around me; dressed in green aprons they jump on their only foot while clapping in the air with their gilded capes; dressed in emerald hats, they are aroused by the locusts in heat, and, before my eyes, the union of two incompatible natures took place.

Fascinated by the crazy ecosystem, I was lying helpless on the ground, my eyes wide open, hungry for images and drunk on oxygen.

The insatiable woman deliriously dug the scene in order to wake up the inhabitants of the earth's center; the newly invited joined the dancers and a deafening round of insects and greenery took place above the music. Mosses, affectionate ants, pink worms, fat plants, starving ferns, tiger beetles, maybugs, multicolored carabid beetles, medlar fruit bouquets, pistils, clovers,

Colorado beetles and bluish buds were entwined to an enchanting music: the Hymn to Life! The locusts rubbed their golden wing sheaths, the cicadas sang their hearts out, the sunflowers juggled between the highs and the lows, the gastrulas gurgled, the lazy moths snored, and on a frosty spring, a praying mantis played the triangle. Oboes in the tree branches, strings in the wild tropical creepers, horns in my body, little bells in the chaste trees, trombones in the long-limbed stems, magical flutes in solitary reeds, the orchestra provided the rhythm and far-off mermaids echoed the song. Suddenly, the earth gave cesarean birth to a black monster, fluid and stinking: a wave of tar shot out from under the dancers' feet and rose up like concrete, hard and impassable.

The coleopteran beetles hushed and the Swiss march ceased its drumming; there we were fearfully contemplating our destruction. Drunk and carefree, we had sipped from Medea's cup and now the sap of the autumn crocuses ran through our poisoned veins. Bit by bit, the tar was invading the forest, imprisoning dancers and musicians in conical tombs. The roses were nothing more than sad black stones, the ceremony had abruptly stopped, a stranger had interrupted the joy and shielded our senses from the sun.

The crusted trees groaned for a last time and the horrible grimace of regret for the celebration formed on our lips. We were too happy, we had to pay for it. An asphalt sheath imprisoned the ferns, tarred crinoline encircled the slender and delicate hips of the wheezing flowers, a locust hiding in my hair buzzed like a chastised child while the hollow of my hand sheltered the corpse of a ladybird. Stuck to the ground, I couldn't move, the spider of evil was punishing me by planting its hairy feelers in the depth of my being; the interrupted ecstasy caused a pain that broke open my belly, spilling my naked scarlet entrails like a colony of monstrous flesh. A last glance toward the peaceful and silent clearing, impossible to reach. Only a deformed imprint remained of me: a black body with a gaping stomach.

I was awakening at that moment with the pleasant surprise of a stomach intact; nevertheless I transformed my dream into a sign. A dark omen: during the night, through seductive metaphors, it had led me toward my tragic end: the clearing was my room, sad but tranquil, the forest was what was beyond my walls; the dark form, that clever and tricky shadow, was the real essence of tar which had the power to smother me: the noisy greenhouse held an irresistible attraction, but its soil contained a black monster from which no one could escape. Not even the sun.

This morning no trace of death remains. Escaping with the night, my dreams, my sighs, Death abandoned me with no hope of seeing Her again. You're not equal to the task, whispers my disillusioned swimmer. Zohr is stronger. You're too impatient. My impeccably clean sheet covers the last imaginary embraces from a paradoxical sleep; mysteriously put back in its place, my desk is cluttered with hangers, their triangles and fish hooks intact. My window is ajar, the cord that jammed its handle lying on the ground. A few rays of sunlight mixing with the floor tiles, it's already getting hot. The street is calm. A white veil passes back and forth under my window, three little girls piggyback on a plastic orange crate and play with the feet of a table busted up by time. No men for the moment. No desire either. Just a few old men at their games under the weeping branches of a fifty-year-old plane tree. The unusually empty trolley crosses the road without even stopping. Under my window, a white veil is still going back and forth, a hand in a pocket marks the first minutes of dawn. Behind lace curtains, more transparent than usual, girls in the neighboring houses smooth back their hair. In the distance I hear the chant of a solitary saint. Standing up like dark blocks, the Atlas peaks protect the desert from the city; the Turaeg are already walking, not worrying about a poor girl condemned to the stake. The street is calm. It looks hot outdoors, elsewhere, separate.

I lift up my nightgown, trembling a bit and suspicious but very quickly a little disappointed. My intact sex appears in a new light: Irony. It defies the room, objects, surprise, the question. Is it the same as yesterday, the day before yesterday, is it the sex from my mothers womb? Yes, it's the same. Pure, virgin. The sex of an adolescent girl on the body of an adolescent girl. A traitorous sex, cared for, ready to receive a stranger, ready to satisfy pride, hope and the expectation of the family, an obsessive sex which disturbs the youth of girls, the dreams of men, a coveted sex, desired and imagined but rarely satisfied. Center of the silhouette, epicenter of pleasure, today it displays its malice by shining with all of its fires like a sewn-on emblem that I can't rip from its breastplate. There, I lie dying on my bed, my mouth dry, and my arms hanging down at my sides with as my only company the sacred coat of arms, the national flag, the black hairnet crest!

The street is now deserted, the old men have left their plane tree; the little girls their chance toy. Nothing is left but a mournful and monotonous chant, that of cloistered girls, requiem to emptiness, the tragic and now the useless. What are our windows, our curtains and our shutters going to be used for? Nothing more to look at, nothing more to wait for, nothing more to hear. Death's melody falls down from the walls, runs on the macadam street, then, also fleeing, it leaves to join up with the deserters. Stretched by a puzzling light, the street extends all the way to the port. The view is clear, the horizon, rid of its cumbersome forms, gives up its secret without fear or modesty: the Port. Earth's last advance, no man's land from nowhere, timeless place of passage, ultimate moment, unreal female who bore me, pause between nothing and nothing, border of nothingness, horrible emptiness, the port is the last prison rampart. Workers embark, disembark, tie up, pile up suitcases, baskets, bags, packages; some sleep on old carts of exile, others have made a nest of sleep for themselves in the corner of a pitch coated wharf. The men leave. They leave us. Abandonment. The final quay. Irremediable decision. In solemn silence they form a chain in solidarity between the earth and the sea, neither scuffles nor cries, just a murmur:

that of desolation. The boats open their greedy mouths and the black mops of hair, hand in hand, climb into the windowless and womanless vessel, fear in their bundles of goods, hope on the other side of the sea. A few arms wave above the bridge railings, and anonymous farewells die in the exquisite light of a timeless day.

Tired of waiting, exhausted witnesses, the men of the street have left my street. The girls of the closed windows stay there, the only faithful ones, sorrowful and guilty companions of the fleeing men; today, the song of the weeping Moorish women is curiously dedicated to those who disturb sleep, celebrations and acts, to the exiles from the country of misfortune and of isolation, to the fearful runaways, hunted down by divine law and always reaching for an ultimate hope of rest, a last safe haven.

And I began to pray with them.

On my knees before my window, I mixed prayers addressed directly to God with my chant; I didn't implore his grace only for myself, I especially wanted him to deliver these poor little girls from hell. My tears garbled my words. Helpless, I was only able to emit the howl of a mad dog, sprawled on the tile flooring, demanding, proud of his complaints, unhappy about his next defeat. How could God understand these throaty sounds, empty of meaning, how could he have comforted a hysterical girl rolling at his feet, a victim of forced solitude, obsessed by her sex? I wished that all of that were only a dream, the houses, the street, the cries, the man in the car, the locked up Saracen women, I wished that I could reach my painting again, the forsaken plain, the frame and its immovable sky! In my turn, I was going to leave. I could not abandon my companions before knowing what real ties united us. I had to know. They had to know. Our tears, our anguish, the tragedy. My hate and their faces. We were there in the same street with a derisive house number as the only thing separating us. Derisively different. The men were no longer from this neighborhood, so we could open our windows, our hands, our mouths. Nothing. What good is it anyway. God is neither compassionate anatomist nor sex exorcist.

Suddenly, my house began to move. The window banged, the swimmer, overcome by shaking, tore a corner of her picture, her head in empty space, she gave me one last sign of pity. It was coming from my door. Someone was violently knocking against the wooden door of my little room. I opened. Clenched palms, hateful and doubtful, a self-satisfied look and complicitous smiles faced me. My mother and Aunt K. were standing at the entrance to my refuge, both impassive and impatient, black and joyful. Zohr was right behind them, her arms loaded with a pitcher full of water, a razor placed on a towel folded in four, and cornered between her throat and her chin a jar of henna. That was it. My hour had sounded without my even hearing it, without my even noticing the union between the big and the little hands. In Zohr's shadow I recognized a tall harsh woman who murmured to me in passing: "I let the man do my work. Damned work! I'll see you soon."

Like three doctor-torturers the women formed a circle around me; one of them was careful to push the door shut and draw the curtains. My mother made me sit on the bed, brutally took off my nightgown and carelessly tore the elastic band from my hair. My hair tousled, my face flushed, my thighs dangling, I allow them to operate. No taste for revolt, just that of a bitter tear in the back of my throat. Aunt K. lifted up my two arms, Zohr moistened my armpits and the cold blind razor blade ran over my body, slowing down on its most private parts. All of a sudden, I became a child again and cursed the little piece of slit skin that sneered at my expense, a simple stroke of the magic blade and my sex found its youth of yesteryear, golden and chubby with a mocking smile marking a very distinct line between its two lips.

My mother spread my hands in the shape of a fan with big red stays, on my palms and the backs of my hands she applied the good luck liquid, then the orange stuff colored the bottom of my feet, accompanied by a delicious tickling sensation that made my chest quiver. Even my chest had passed under the lawnmower, the little black comma-shaped hairs, flatter than the rest of my body and which formerly encircled my nipples, had disappeared, an invisible needle had pierced my breast flesh here and there and everywhere, and I discovered between my two breasts the pointed end of a hair that remembers.

During the long summer cleaning the women were talking. And by way of a few insipid sentences, I learned what the real necessity was, strictly speaking, yet "more than enough": the heart of my next story.

— Yes! he's rich!
— Mabrouk, my daughter, Mabrouk!*
— Mister Bachir of course!
— The idiotic car! the car...
— It's said he waited seven days and seven nights.
— Time enough for a tale to be told!
— I am proud, proud, proud!
— Tomorrow, if God wishes, the big celebration!
— Good, very good.
— He's rich, very rich!
— Mabrouk! yooyooyooyooyooyooyooyooyooyoo!
— You're the most beautiful, my daughter, the most beautiful!
— Yooyooyooyooyooyooyooyooyooyoo!
— Mabrouk alik!*

That's how they ripped me from my solitude.

The job finished, the women looked at me proudly. It was clean. Spotless. However they didn't notice the small rumbling becoming a sob that will whimper before transforming into a tear. Right

---

*Mabrouk: congratulations
*Mabrouk alik!: congratulations to you!

there, trapped between my thorax and my stomach. They were careful to lock the door, and I lay down a last time on my child's bed, stripped and abandoned. The curtains were closed. The show, too.

Today: adverb designating the day where one is. Laughable definition, when today is not a reference point but a simple reminder of yesterday, identical to the day before yesterday and tomorrow. Time flees today and today flees time. Bilateral contract. Impossible to break it. The present is not more than the past, and we who aspire to melt into the past, smashed by its artificial tentacles always stretched toward an imaginary future, we don't exist either. A shadow in the shadow of hours, infinitely small in the infinitely large, today is the day where I am not. The battle of minutes has stopped; pulled along by the immobile chariot of seconds, I find myself in a space amputated from its time, its only sign a thin thread of light.

However "today" detaches itself from its counterparts. It has form, body, soul and reality thanks to a new function: finality. I am going to leave my house, my neighbors and my child's bed; during the night, the event marked a big "E" across my forehead and it's in a conscious state that I descended the stairs, ready to embrace tragedy and its friend the ultimate. And trembling a little, certainly, but happy about the arrival of a new story, forgetting even that *I* was its main and necessary ingredient!

The sum of accumulated days exploded into a formidable abstraction that filled the whole of my perceptible framework. There was but one day left, this day, to be precise. An interlude between boredom and boredom, I had to live it very attentively in order to hold on to a few scrimptions of color until the next one. A Moslem woman leaves her house twice: for her marriage and for her funeral. Or so tradition had decreed. Concentrated on things, my gestures and all of my thoughts, I was becoming my own witness, and by an involuntary effort I was watching myself embrace the adventure. Objects had put on death's veil, before the hour, I was attending and participating in a joyous funeral: my own. I was burying my childhood in order to go live beyond it, myself and the known.

The living room, disfigured by a veritable cataclysm, was transformed into a ballroom. The mutation of said place occurred during the night. The event marked another "E" across the protective curtain. Pouf cushions, pillows, tables, couch pulled out for the occasion opened up the view to a clever and malicious juggling between *trompe-l'oeil* and reality; in this big space, the author of the tragedy never lost track of the appropriate characters, each in his place. Center, nooks and crannies, blind or voyeuristic angles, mobile furniture, silk, sequins, little silver bells moving in hip-shifting rhythm, pointed shoes, net stockings and fleshy arms, golden volcanoes flowing over moist low-cut dresses, faces done up in three colors from eyes to chin, party sparkles, gossiping mouths, smiles twisted and frozen, profiles of monkey and goddess, masks, old fogies, fineries and making the appearance, shining brocade and satin, fat or transparent forms, from chubby to anemic, the gold-horde is replete!

Unfolding their emerald peacock feathers, displaying stones and period-piece bracelets, proud, retiring or given to gossip, the Moorish women take up the whole of my living room. I hadn't realized the enormity of my family! Nieces, aunts, girl cousins, great aunts, smaller aunts, mothers, mothers-in-law, grandmothers, dressers, make-up artists, musicians, eaters, female voyeurs, weepers, the full feminine palette from the East, the West, the North, and the South of Algiers is gathered in my honor. What an honor! Shy lips and greedy mouths, fat and bulgy stomachs, an out-of-tune orchestra plays the famous symphony of the insane farmyard! Jaws clatter in the overly perfumed air while the oldest Saracen women, attached to the wall like old tapestries brought out for the celebration, clap their callused and memory-laden hands.

Tradition is a vengeful lady against whom I cannot fight. It was like this for them, it will be like this for the others. Repetitive movement inquiring neither about time nor my refusal, and even less about our youth. A change of decor, return to more of the same chanted in a monotone. Your turn, Fikria! Today it's me. Me, me, me! My whole being bears the adventure, bears up under it, I am its nursing mother, the epicenter, the tourist brochure that curious and examining hands finger in every sense. Crumple up. The sacred stone kissed by superstitious mouths. The last night of the condemned. A living good luck charm, white and orange on the palm of my hands, with two black circles under my eyes, recalling the former color of my sex. Don't you get it? I bring bad luck!

Resigned, worn out, sick at heart, violated, wounded in the armpits, irritated between my thighs, I offer no resistance, welcoming with neither joy nor pain the anonymous compliments and the heavy sound of the derbouka droning for me. A small box with open bottom, decorated on the sides with Kabyle figurines, that's this evening's source of rhythm.

Eager to know what's going on, I step aside from the moist circle of dancers so I can look at the guilty one. My mother proudly waltzes among her women friends, her enemies, and her sisters for one night, her hair is in delicate braids, tucked into a heavy bun, the auburn crop wisely stays above her head like the crown of a queen being anointed. Powdered from head to foot, cheered up by the approaching victory, in ecstasy before the party buffet, the "inter-course," smug with contentment, my mother, my very dear mother avoids my eyes; she flies, spins around, flits about, she counts, adds, will there be enough table settings, enough room, enough joy? She shines like a nugget of gold in the middle of a slimy spring, jingle jingle go her mother's bracelets hung on coarse wrists and frigid ankles, jingle jingle go the bracelets which will later ring in my trembling hands.

The old Moorish woman, out of breath, bloated by overly greasy cakes and idleness, has found her former youth, laughing sneeringly, criticizing, on the look out, swearing, she whirls about like a frightened wasp around the honey of the new story, reborn, she seems to be the bride for one evening. Forgetting her inhuman forms, everyone is there to congratulate her. Me, I'm hidden behind the half-open kitchen door. Nobody sees me except for a little plump hand playing with the sections of my excessively long dress: frightened Leyla. A projection of myself onto my mother. A projection of my mother onto me. I feel my sex lubricate. Out of fear. Waiting for the event, the grasshopper hops around her guests, boasting about her daughter's qualities, the only fertile one in the house, "She loves me, she respects me, she'll never disappoint me, she's fragrant like the spring air," and I answer, "I'm fragrant like frustration perfuming the pants of men in the street, Mamma, I cut you to pieces with kisses. And murderous thoughts!"

Jingle jingle go the cymbals in your kitchen. Common woman! There you are united for life to another sister: my mother-in-law. Fat sister! All dressed up like an old woman, she is twenty years older than my mother, has a fat son and gilded tooth stumps that dazzle in the darkness of the overcrowded living room, in the Most Dark of my thoughts; her hind-quarters wrinkled by an oriental crinoline cloth, her package body seems fatter to me, her hips wider than those of the female who bore me, unless it's the wide shape of her dress, which gives her a conical and hardly seductive silhouette. Apparent nobility, cellulite-armored thighs, diamond-covered social climber, bolted shut sex and vulture's eye, jingle jingle go my mother-in-law's red claws on the porcelain plates. I hear my pulse throughout the whole house. It's getting frantic. I cajole it. My breasts have heartburn. The night rumbles. The derbouka goes into heat. Musical notes grope the curtains. Sound drools from the windows. The celebration begins!

One excited female, unable to hold back any longer, takes off her pumps, lets down her hair and rushes forth onto a dance floor of her own invention. Inauguration of the monster merry-go-round. Her "spare-tire" stomach, egged on by the applause of the other women, gets worked up under the transparent silk, two bowling ball breasts jump and jerk in between the embroidered designs of the traditional costume, the professional Moorish woman swings her stomach from right to left, from left to right, then, no longer distinguishing the left from the right, she makes it do a complete circle above the uncarpeted tiling; roused by the sudden leaps and bounds of her companion, her pussy, it opens itself up in front of us. Spreading apart, two little reddish-brown pillows: leathery wrinkled jewel box of crimson sheathing fore-wings. Sweating like an animal tracked by hunters, it gesticulates, complains, declaims, clamors its furor to the liberating males. Too bad Leyla doesn't have a prick. To her great despair! Just two bowed legs about as good as a dried-up well. In an unknown room the Saracen men, distanced from their dissimilars, finger the beads of time by downing little yellow glasses overflowing with aniseed alcohol. They smoke, they talk loudly and slap their thighs, they dance and they caress each other. In an unknown waiting room my father negotiates the future with a masked face. Strange meeting of two foreign alliances. The sad women content themselves with a pair of breasts in the form of bowling balls and rejoin the unsatisfied female in a round of cellulite and bitterness. The youngest keep rhythm by banging their silver bracelets together. The oldest, already exhausted, comment joyously on the ballet of the infantile women. Laughs, winks, tricks, pretenses, ululations, kisses, bodies brushing, pleasure-seeking women among women seeking pleasure, the female lovers with disappointed sex embrace each other with eyes closed.

Leaning against a wall I squeeze the hand of my little sister's who's standing up with one leg wrapped around my calf, the other balancing, and I watch the sad show. It's enough to make you weep. In a grotesque dance, the madness and despair of an entire people was being embodied. Symbolic signs of the most constrained stage-whisper, the dance and the joy did not mix the sexes. A wedding should recall a precedent and call out to a successor. And here? Absurd wedding rigged by female-males and male-females. In her turn Leyla gesticulated against my thigh, just missing making me fall. Ape who apes her she-ape, annoyed I sent her rolling onto the floor.

Zohr, the sickly plant, is hiding behind the still deserted buffet, ugliness has been posed as if by magic between a wall of wisteria and a rectangular table; mixed in with the flowers and the meat, she doesn't disturb. It is definitely Zohr. Definitely. A colorless dress matched with a headdress made in the same material envelops the pile of bones sparkling weakly thanks to a big brooch pinned to her heart; the little hairy and angular weasel head pokes out of Zohr's veil to jealously survey her companion. Curled up in a cherry basket, Death, momentarily dozing in her arms, dreams of the collective eschatology and leaves Zohr a few minutes of pleasure. My sister claps her veined hands, stiff and tense, dry and rough. Out-of-sync finger snapping, unfamiliar with the derbouka and the ululations of the excited women, emitting only hateful and cold musical trills that kill youth and hope. Zohr is not a dupe. Zohr is weak. Zohr is sick. Nobody sees her. Nobody hears her going after her nails and fingers like a nut case. Wallflower, she chews a stray piece of meat, her meal for the evening, and her lips, as frosty as a tombstone of the great North, I see a little blood-worm running: a smile in full hemorrhage.

Our glances intersect, collide, bang and congeal. Joined again by a foot bridge where an unfathomable countryside embeds itself on the two sides of the rock, link between nothingness and

94

Life, juncture between the logical and the absurd, our eyes question each other. Who is who? Her white pupils reflect the image of my soul ruined by submission. I'm not a dupe either. Deceased for a long time inside, dried out on the outside, I'm like you Zohr. You just have a little edge on me, in addition to practice, that's all. Life is a female thief. I have stolen your place, put on your clothes, made your skin into my skin, made your sex into my sex. You're the older one, so Mister Bachir should have aimed his index finger at you. And what do you make of this odor of blood smoking between my thighs?

Death has its whims that reason has not.

The heavy strong perfume of the white flowers falls onto my shoulders like the brilliant guillotine blade, the August moths flutter around the sun-queen, pitying the future female traveler, their wings, irritated by the walls, make of them prisoners of the wisteria bunches, a wreath falls at my feet, I pick it up and wrap it around my neck; moribund female, embarked on the boat of judgment, I go down the Euphrates river, my arms held out toward the masked face of my commander. I want to flee, but the female guardians of the joyful fortress are vigilant, thrilled with the final verdict, they dance to the glory of the executioner, entrenched for the moment in a cell that resembles mine. Outside, I hear the cloistered girls gnawing on their window frames, stepping over the roadway, and, like hungry leeches, they glue themselves to the keyholes of my closed soul. What were they seeing? A complicated mechanics of tangled up vessels, of whitish-colored organs, soft and malleable, separated by an inviolable gate made of the iron of eternal return, of habit, of memory, and of tradition.

I want to flee, Leyla is forever nailed to the floor, my mother wanted to sew closed my vulva, the ashes of a cadaver block Zohr's veins, the derbouka drones, a woman is unwell, there is blood on her dress, Ourdhia was bitten by a snake, my father betrayed my secret, Mister Bachir will be watchful, I won't bring along my swimmer, she will die on the wall while I will die between the thighs of an old man. My dress is imprinted with the heads of miniature rats. Following the rhythm of my gestures they smile or show their teeth. It all depends. The mood displayed for the moment changes when time stretches or retracts; slave of the minutes, I have made a pocket between my waist and a gold-piece belt, there, I stuff the souvenir of my last moments.

Laid out on a bed of potatoes, garlic, parsley and red herbs, legs in the air, thighs immobile, sexes stuffed, stomachs gaping and eyes half-closed, grease spread around like wax, and lots of flesh, the *méchoui* waits for the devastating fingers. Decapitated in my honor in an empty bathtub, then full of blood and senses, the sheep seem to sleep peacefully far from the city, far from the celebration, far from my sadness; dozing in time's shadow in a foreign land whose borders we will never know, they deliver only one phrase of their secret: a derisively dead body. Having fled through the ceiling windows of my mother's blast furnaces, the spirits waltz in the Invisible and sometimes stop the farcical merry-go-round of nothingness so they can aim a few little arrows at me, which whistle in a wind of irony and bitterness. Under the scalped heads hangs a piece of lace-like black bloody flesh, made irregular, and full of holes on the sides, by an awkward knife; posed as a macabre decoration on each end of the trays, the heads look at me with wide-open white eyes: "Poor Fikria, how ridiculous you look with your dress that is too long and your little shoulders that carry the heavy burden of a useless youth! Catastrophic balance sheet, entering days and days of sadness mixed with dead times: springboard for an even more frightening solitude, solitude with two then with three, four, five, maybe eight!"

---

mechoui: a whole lamb roasted on a spit

Blood no longer flows in my veins, only little droplets of despair. They fall from my heart, make furrows in my entrails and pearl on my forehead, they blur space, block the horizon and dwarf my future.

I am no more than a flower without petals soaking in a vase of gray water, the vase of bitterness.

Bathed in perspiration, the women have stopped dancing. The derbouka is still droning, but the sounds show themselves to be heavier, spaced so far apart that they are as if visible to the naked eye. They mark the beat to show just how solemn the hour is. The death knoll has sounded in the house of closed windows. Like mechanical dolls, the waltzers leave the turning pedestal to put their shoes back on; vivaciously clapping the air the devastating fingers heat up, and they cling to the bloody buffet: open season has been declared!

Musk, amber, henna, wisteria, jasmine, mint, anise mix together in soup plates, melt in the clay jars, are drunk from multicolored goblets; Muscat grapes adorn the copper platters, the buckwheat cakes crumble onto the tile floor, silvery wreaths, squeezed lemons, suras from the Koran, pearls of sweat, jars of lemonade, semolina, tea, coffee, grains, oils, sea salt, peppery powder, stuffed peppers, smelly underarms, fabrics, silk, undone hairdos, joy, laughter, crystal dishes, a veil of perfumes, of images, of gestures and of harvested words, stand up between Zohr and me, between me and Zohr. The sickly plant observes the massacre, and still, still, no one sees her.

Expert hands greet in passing the heads poked full of garlic, they dive into a little cup of sacred water to cleanse themselves, then hover in the empty space like the wings of a vulture above open coffins; impatient but embarrassed by the abundance, the devastating fingers bless the spread out flesh, dead, helpless in the sauce between bouquets of fragrant herbs, the fingers hesitate, go around, fly over, avoid, change direction, play with a stalk of parsley, scratch a piece of the tablecloth, pinch a cup handle: indecent feast in the country of want, the indecency of a violated tomb.

Finally, carried away by hunger, the fingers fight without restraint on tombs open to the public, stirring up earth and dandelions, groping beneath the displaced slab, exposing the most private flesh to the light. A swarm of painted nails buries itself in the dark countryside of a gaping stomach, bangs against a skin stretched out from cooking, explores the least appetizing parts and grabs on desperately to a rump stuffed with large meatballs.

After having soaked in the sauce, the blood, the flesh and the grease, the fingers, reddened by the spices, valiantly transport their prey to the bottom of a cold throat; devourers of dead things, the busy Moorish women chew on the overcooked meats and with the stroke of a forked tongue catch the little pieces of cadavers stuck on their "pneumatic" lips. Congregated around the rectangular coffin, they shove each other, lick, make holes, swallow, smother each other, rip, shear, suck, spray themselves, cut off pieces, quench their thirst, and in a shared burp they digest death!

Diamonds are lost in the garnishes, bracelets scrape the trays, the silk clothing is stained, veined hands pierce sheaths of skin, and the dismembered sheep again stand up straight above the slab like wild-looking creatures on the point of death.

During this time, the children, macabre anatomists, made games out of the sheep knuckle bones.

The feast having ended, I returned to my room to put on my wedding dress. The last dress. Slipped on in a child's room, later it will become wrinkled on an unknown armchair, in the shadow of sighs and the final cry, like the critical witness of two foreign moments: Before. After! It is long and mauve-colored, puffed out on the forearms, it flares at calf level. A flounce bordered by a black line finishes its cut, golden threads burst out from its elastic gathers. It isn't really beautiful, yet hardly had I put it on than I found it irresistibly attractive. It covered up the last shivers of a fearful body, and in its folds sadness, fear and regret huddled. The seams alone contained my emotions, its wide form and its loose-fitting look protected my past thoughts. I knew that while putting it away in the cupboard of my new room, it would inevitably evoke the memory of a present time close by. I made a second skin out of this dress, a double of my body that would continue to live, hung on a hanger, robbed of its head, animated by empty forms, impregnated with an old smell, I made of it my second memory.

I still have a few minutes left to contemplate my room. I concentrate on the objects so I can extract a detail, a fault or a quality, an odor or a color, a little nothing which I will jealously guard deep inside of me until the end of time.

The curtains, the stool, my bed of pleasure, the bathroom, the little cruel lamp, all of these insignificant things took on life and questioned me. Sentimental, I answered by giving them affectionate nicknames. Decorations of my solitude, inanimate accomplices, female voyeurs, props for my imagination, I covered them with kisses, and, with a light touch of the hand, my objects became brilliant lights! I falsified my memories, and in the present moment all that I had cursed grouped together in a block of emotions.

Masquerading under a new title, I had to leave my child's room. Pulled by the future, torn apart by the repetitive and by tradition, I already lay dying in regrets. These hours of boredom, this hospital odor, the dusty greenhouse, these invisible hands which disturbed me at night, the deceitful window, the cold tiling warmed by the first dawn's sun, my little swimmer, the bus that does not come, the crowded sidewalk, the minutes that would grip the curtains . . . . In a whirlwind of banal images, everything methodically returned and I already mourned for my enemies! Embellished by a hardly faithful memory, the old relics shined in the room of one thousand and one pains; I declared them to be privileged witnesses of my childhood and sent them to God's throne to be sanctified.

Like a shedding animal, I left them my first skin as a present, my being and my breath.

The celebrating women cluck in the staircase. My mother rushes into my room without knocking, her hateful presence suddenly sweeps away all of my thoughts. The last images of a fabricated reminiscence were dying on the tiling. Soon it is going to be night. Aunt K. grabs my head of hair and for a last time smooths it back with the roughness common to all of the women of her sort. Zohr applies a layer of gaudy bright red finger nail polish; underneath her skin, one could hear Death galloping around. The three women speed up time. A little made-up girl pulled on her dress to hide calves that were too thin. They retouch the make-up, soften the juvenile imperfections, brighten up the color, accentuate the features with a dark color, two spots of henna mark my forehead as the branding iron marks sheep, and in my veins my heart was rebelling.

The gold mixes with the silver, my wrists jingle with foreign materials, brilliant stones are hung on my earlobes then reddened by the pressure of precious leech-like stones, an agate necklace encircles my neck, my ankles are fettered by coral anklets, a Southern cross dangles between two uneven fleshy growths. I think of Ourdhia and I cry. Zohr says that it's because of the kohl. Other women join us, thrilled, they contemplate the bride and her ornaments, congratulate once more the female who bore me and reach their hands out toward my unrecognizable face. They caress my dress material forgetting that, underneath, a child breathes; when the devastating fingers encountered my overly narrow hips — the shape of an unfinished jar — I breathed in another smell: the perfume of embarrassment and confusion. The deceitfulness was obvious, but nobody dared to pity the little girl. That's how it was. They had hated their mothers for it, but time fogs memory, and other girls were preparing themselves in a child's room.

Like lascivious hired mourners, the Moorish women recited the first suras of the Koran so as to be pardoned by a remote God who scorns them, and for the first time watching a voyeur-woman felt herself being looked at, but it was too late! On the other side of the sea, the bells celebrated the funeral of a newborn.

Thanks to you, Mamma, I will be a perfect spouse for Mister Bachir. I will know how to disappear at the right moment, hidden in the kitchen I will hold back my tears and my legs which will want to run into the forest, a smile will be there like a fly hanging onto a piece of spoiled meat, fixed on my mouth, it will falsely liven up the face that you gave me, I will fix my hair like you, I will cover my shoulders with the veil of modesty and respect, the years will pass by without really passing, my hips will carry the fruits of nature, I will satisfy my spouse's desires, even on the tile flooring of a dark little kitchen, I will hide when he is dining and I will cry when he falls asleep, my blood will honor our family's blood and I will cry only out of pain. This pain that will no longer be mine. I have remembered my lesson, my sex is shaved, my breasts are almost ready, I have erased the last traces of a long sob, I know how to make cakes, I have forgotten my fears and my boredom, the window will be closed, my mind too, no memories, no regrets, I will pray to God to pardon me and will bridle my passions. I forget that I am nothing but a belly for reproduction, and I preciously guard your bracelets for my poor little girls.

The sun replaces sadness. The night puts anguish to sleep. Thank you Mamma!

Escorted by the women, I go down the staircase taking care not to stumble. Veiled, I have only one eye left to count the last seconds which transport me to the last instant. The essence of the adventure flowed from the walls, and at the foot of the walls rolled dark tears. The front door opens. A suicidal moth scorches its wings on burning embers. I hear the car door creak, a delivery van, transformed into a mobile garden, waits. At the center of the event, I went forward into the night, one-eyed and resigned, toward the death vehicle. On the second floor, behind a closed window, a little hand was waving a white flag. Zohr explodes on the derbouka, the women cry out with joy for the last time, waking up the longshoremen at the port. Pushed by my mother, I am engulfed by the metallic lair; I had just enough time to catch an accusatory look and a black door closed again on my veil. A bulb hanging from the ceiling lights up the locked up-box, rose and wisteria wreaths cover the bench for two, the windows are filled in with triangular pieces of cardboard, an iron plate separates me from the driver. A shaking set the motor into motion, and, surrounded by flowers, I headed for a new story.

A pack of dogs trailed behind the van.

About the Author

Nina Bouraoui was born in Rennes, France, on July 31, 1967, of an Algerian father and French mother. Shortly thereafter, she moved to Algiers with her family where she stayed until the age of thirteen. During the rest of her adolescence, her family lived in Switzerland and the United Arab Emirates. She attended French *lycées* and finally moved to Paris to pursue her university studies. She studied law for two years, then philosophy for another two years, during which time she worked on the present book, her first novel, *La Voyeuse interdite,* begun at the age of nineteen and finished when she was twenty-three.

The story of Nina Bouraoui's publication with Editions Gallimard, one of the most renowned French presses, is rather extraordinary, or as she terms it, a real fairy tale. She had been writing since she was young—a personal journal, short stories, poems—but it was only at the age of nineteen that she decided to write a complete novel. When it was finished, she found the addresses of the best-known presses in her Paris telephone book and sent her unsolicited manuscript, with no agent as intermediary, to Gallimard. Three days later, the editors responded positively. In 1991, she received the literary prize, *Prix du Livre Inter,* and went on to establish a record for her first novel: 140,000 copies sold. She continues to write and has the luxury of so few writers: she lives by her writing.

Nina Bouraoui grew up in a liberal university milieu, completely unlike the one she describes in *Forbidden Vision*. Because of the strength of her memories, both good and bad, of her years spent in Algeria, and her own Algerian roots, she wanted her first novel to be about that country. Eager to portray Algerian society and character as she describes them—"boiling," "dangerous," "exciting"—she does acknowledge how very difficult it is to be a woman in Algeria. Although the story itself is important, Bouraoui emphasizes that it is not directly autobiographical, but consists of a composite of stories heard, anecdotes, and an acknowledgment of the extreme sexual tensions felt by both women and men in Algeria because of the segregation of the sexes and their respective roles, still dictated to a great degree by traditional norms. There is a foundation of truth in the story which does not intend to mask Bouraoui's main themes: the lack of communication between human beings, solitude, and the resulting suffering of both men and women.

She draws upon a collective memory of how life was, and in many cases still is, for women in Algeria. She feels, too, perhaps paradoxically, given the violence depicted in *Forbidden Vision*, that as Westerners we should not be too judgmental about what we perceive to be the slowness with which Algerian society is evolving in its treatment of women—this even in light of the current political, religious and social crises in Algeria.

For Bouraoui, style and the craft of writing are important beyond the content of the story. Her care in evoking very particular colors, sensations, odors, fragrances, moods, and feelings is evident in the energetic play of language, striking images and deliberate exaggeration. Speaking of her writing, she says:

> I am a female voyeur; nothing escapes me, neither odors, colors, nor breaths. I steal certain details from reality and propel them into another reality: that of my characters. Words and wrongs surround me, I need only hold out my hand to seize them. An author is a character with two faces. I oscillate between the true and false, between reality and illusion.

Her second novel, *Poing mort*, was also published by Gallimard, in 1992. She is now at work on a third.

ABOUT THE TRANSLATOR

K. Melissa Marcus is an Assistant Professor of French at Northern Arizona University in Flagstaff. She holds a B.A. in French and Political Science (1978) and an M.A. in Political Science (1981), both from the University of California, Santa Barbara, and a Ph.D. in French from Stanford University (1990).

TRANSLATOR'S ACKNOWLEDGMENTS

In 1991, I discovered Nina Bouraoui's work while doing research in Paris. I quickly became enamored of the story and intrigued that the author had already developed such a strong voice despite her youth. Since *Forbidden Vision* was my first literary translation, I was particularly concerned with accurately rendering into English the richness and varied texture of the French original. Several characteristics presented a difficult challenge. For example, Bouraoui writes in different registers and often shifts abruptly from one to the other. She is serious, sarcastic, sad, angry, and graphic in her descriptions. As a translator, I had to understand the subtleties of mood and context expressed in all of these shifts before I could decide how to express the same in English. Another challenge throughout the text is the alternation of third and first person narrative voices. Furthermore, the line between reality, dream, and fantasy is not always apparent. Fortunately, I was able to correspond regularly with the author. She very willingly clarified difficult passages and answered all of my queries. After finishing several drafts of my translation, I finally had the fortune to meet and interview Nina Bouraoui in Paris during the summer of 1994. She is a young but nevertheless very serious and dedicated writer who passionately works at her craft. I would like to thank Nina Bouraoui for her time and for graciously allowing me to interview her.